PRAI

Tom Clancy fans open to a strong female lead will clamor for more.

— *Drone*, Publishers Weekly

Superb!

— *Drone*, Booklist starred review

The best military thriller I've read in a very long time. Love the female characters.

— *Drone*, Sheldon McArthur, founder of The Mystery Bookstore, LA

A fabulous soaring thriller.

— *Take Over at Midnight*, Midwest Book Review

Meticulously researched, hard-hitting, and suspenseful.

— *Pure Heat*, Publishers Weekly, starred review

Expert technical details abound, as do realistic military missions with superb imagery that will have readers feeling as if they are right there in the midst and on the edges of their seats.

— *LIGHT UP THE NIGHT,* RT REVIEWS, 4 1/2 STARS

Buchman has catapulted his way to the top tier of my favorite authors.

— FRESH FICTION

Nonstop action that will keep readers on the edge of their seats.

— *TAKE OVER AT MIDNIGHT,* LIBRARY JOURNAL

M L. Buchman's ability to keep the reader right in the middle of the action is amazing.

— LONG AND SHORT REVIEWS

The only thing you'll ask yourself is, "When does the next one come out?"

— *WAIT UNTIL MIDNIGHT,* RT REVIEWS, 4 STARS

The first...of (a) stellar, long-running (military) romantic suspense series.

I knew the books would be good, but I didn't realize how good.

Buchman mixes adrenalin-spiking battles and brusque military jargon with a sensitive approach.

13 times "Top Pick of the Month"

THE COMPLETE US COAST GUARD

A MILITARY ROMANTIC SUSPENSE STORY
COLLECTION

M. L. BUCHMAN

Buchman Bookworks

Other works by M. L. Buchman: *(* - also in audio)*

Thrillers

Dead Chef
Swap Out!
One Chef!
Two Chef!

Miranda Chase
Drone*
Thunderbolt*
Condor*

Romantic Suspense

Delta Force
Target Engaged*
Heart Strike*
Wild Justice*
Midnight Trust*

Firehawks
MAIN FLIGHT
Pure Heat
Full Blaze
Hot Point*
Flash of Fire*
Wild Fire
SMOKEJUMPERS
Wildfire at Dawn*
Wildfire at Larch Creek*
Wildfire on the Skagit*

The Night Stalkers
MAIN FLIGHT
The Night Is Mine
I Own the Dawn
Wait Until Dark
Take Over at Midnight
Light Up the Night
Bring On the Dusk
By Break of Day

AND THE NAVY
Christmas at Steel Beach
Christmas at Peleliu Cove
WHITE HOUSE HOLIDAY
Daniel's Christmas*
Frank's Independence Day*
Peter's Christmas*
Zachary's Christmas*
Roy's Independence Day*
Damien's Christmas*
5E
Target of the Heart
Target Lock on Love
Target of Mine
Target of One's Own

Shadow Force: Psi
At the Slightest Sound*
At the Quietest Word*

White House Protection Force
Off the Leash*
On Your Mark*
In the Weeds*

Contemporary Romance

Eagle Cove
Return to Eagle Cove
Recipe for Eagle Cove
Longing for Eagle Cove
Keepsake for Eagle Cove

Henderson's Ranch
Nathan's Big Sky*
Big Sky, Loyal Heart*
Big Sky Dog Whisperer*

Love Abroad
Heart of the Cotswolds: England
Path of Love: Cinque Terre, Italy

Other works by M. L. Buchman:

Contemporary Romance (cont)

Where Dreams
Where Dreams are Born
Where Dreams Reside
Where Dreams Are of Christmas
Where Dreams Unfold
Where Dreams Are Written

Science Fiction / Fantasy

Deities Anonymous
Cookbook from Hell: Reheated
Saviors 101

Single Titles
The Nara Reaction
Monk's Maze
the Me and Elsie Chronicles

Non-Fiction

Strategies for Success
Managing Your Inner Artist/Writer
Estate Planning for Authors*
Character Voice
Narrate and Record Your Own
Audiobook*

Short Story Series by M. L. Buchman:

Romantic Suspense

Delta Force
Delta Force

Firehawks
The Firehawks Lookouts
The Firehawks Hotshots
The Firebirds

The Night Stalkers
The Night Stalkers
The Night Stalkers 5E
The Night Stalkers CSAR
The Night Stalkers Wedding Stories

US Coast Guard
US Coast Guard

White House Protection Force
White House Protection Force

Contemporary Romance

Eagle Cove
Eagle Cove

Henderson's Ranch
Henderson's Ranch*

Where Dreams
Where Dreams

Thrillers

Dead Chef
Dead Chef

Science Fiction / Fantasy

Deities Anonymous
Deities Anonymous

Other
The Future Night Stalkers
Single Titles

CONTENTS

ABOUT THIS BOOK

Join M. L. Buchman for this five-story collection about the heroes and heroines of the US Coast Guard.

Praise for M. L.'s military romance series:

- *"The contemporary standard bearer of military romance."*
- *"Top 10 Romance of the Year."*
- *"A romantic adrenaline junkie's kind of book."*

M. L. will lead you through each story with brand-new introductions, their origins, and why they were written.

Discover tales of danger, adventure, and ever-lasting love with the Coast Guard's bravest rescuers.

Five great reads for one amazing price.

INTRODUCTION

I LIVED ON THE OREGON COAST FOR SIX YEARS. LESS THAN half a mile from the lovely and incredibly dangerous shore that stretches three hundred miles from the California border to where the mighty Columbia River separates Oregon from Washington. It is austere, wild, rugged, and *incredibly* dangerous.

Along our town's twenty-mile stretch of coast, we typically lost ten to fifteen people a year. They were mostly tourists who, despite all the warning signs, underestimated the Pacific Ocean. The chill waters demand a wetsuit at any time of year. Hypothermia, rip currents, and a bizarre event called sneaker waves (waves that suddenly inundate an entire beach with no warning) are but a few of the hazards. Tourists playing on the logs, some five feet across and a hundred feet long, don't think about the waves that tossed them there, and would someday take them to sea again. Or the power of the big breakers that might decide to heave such logs into the second story of a beachside hotel (saw that happen a few times).

It's a favorite pastime of inlanders to come to the coast to witness the big storms. They go right down on the beach to see it up close and personal, little realizing that if they're caught by a thirty-foot breaker, nothing will save them. The boom of those monster waves hitting the sand can be heard a mile or more inland.

Even on non-stormy days, tourists are often trapped on sheer cliffs by the massive ten-to-twelve-foot tidal swings. There are locals who can't walk the beach at all in the summer, because they can't stand to see parents letting their kids run into even the standard three-to-six-foot waves unattended.

One of the comforting sounds that makes locals look upward and wave aloft almost every day is the US Coast Guard patrols. Orange HH-65 Dolphin rescue helos run beach patrols above all of the most popular spots and are responsible for saving so many lives.

But that isn't the most dangerous part of the coast. That lies at the Oregon-Washington border where the Columbia River dumps a quarter of a million cubic feet per second into the Pacific (three Olympic pools per second, about seven thousand tons of water). The fifth largest river by discharge in North America, it is a fire hose into the Pacific as it has no delta, just a narrow outlet.

This plows into the chill remnants of the North Pacific Current and storms that can approach from any whimsical direction. They all meet at one of the West Coast's top seaports.

The Columbia River Bar is generally ranked as the worst shipping water anywhere in the world. Nicknamed the "Graveyard of the Pacific", over two thousand shipwrecks have been recorded there since explorers first arrived. It makes Cape Horn at the southern tip of South America appear to be a safe passage.

Therefore, the men and women of the US Coast Guard are there in force. With its own Sector-level headquarters, the mouth of the Columbia boasts: two cutters, three rescue helicopters, and five motor lifeboats aside from the National Motor Lifeboat School (the most prestigious in the world) are all run from there. They respond to hundreds of assistance calls every year. Approximately three hundred personnel are stationed there including the school.

Curiously though, I didn't start writing this series when I lived there.

It took me moving back to the East Coast, which I had left the day after graduating from college, to look all the way back to Oregon. Perhaps it was a bit of homesickness (I lived in the Northwest for almost four decades). Perhaps it was seeing the USCG presence along the North Shore of Massachusetts where I've landed over three thousand miles away. Suddenly, here was the Coast Guard...again.

Founded in 1790, it is the oldest continuous sea-going service in our military (the Navy was disbanded from the end of the Revolutionary War until 1794). While it is the second smallest uniformed service in the US (only the newly formed US Space Force is smaller, at the moment), by itself it is the twelfth largest navy in the world. They safeguard our inland waterways from the Great Lakes and the Mississippi to our coastlines, and have deployed overseas in every major conflict in US history including both World Wars, Korea, Vietnam, and Iraq.

The wonder isn't that I decided to tell some of their stories, it's that it took me so long to do so. But how to grapple with "The Forgotten Service" as it is often called? Especially one so varied.

I decided to focus on one small area: the Columbia River Bar, and the men and women who protect people and shipping there.

CROSSING THE BAR

Carlos Torres agreed to guest host his aunt's Crossing the Bar podcast on a whim. That's how he'd run most of his life to date, so why not.

Petty officer Sarah Goodwin fought long and hard to achieve the rank of US Coast Guard Surfman. It made her the best driver that the National Motor Lifeboat School has trained in years.

Carlos joins her on a training ride, that turns into a desperate rescue in the treacherous waters over the Columbia River Bar. A rescue that charts a new life's course for them both.

INTRODUCTION

This story was inspired by a resident of Astoria, Oregon, Joanne Rideout. In 2004, she became intrigued by all of the ships she saw crossing the Columbia River Bar outside her window. So, she began a podcast (in the same year those were ever called by that name).

This short, typically ten minutes daily, report captures the heart of the shipping in the area. It began as a list of ships but quickly grew to include stories of their crew and their adventures. One poor ship she told of was pirated four separate times in a single voyage enroute to Astoria, leading me to include it in the story below.

I can highly recommend her wonderful creation, *Ship Report,* no matter where you live: https://shipreport.net/.

Little did Ms. Rideout know of the huge popularity her assuaging of her own curiosity would create. It doesn't rival the hundred-and-fifty-year-old *Shipping Forecast* issued daily by the BBC Radio 4, but it probably falls as a solid second worldwide.

But how to combine that with my desire to write about the US Coast Guard?

I then recalled the National Motor Lifeboat School. The very best coxswains from all over the world come here for training in the fierce waters of the Columbia River Bar.

The ones who succeed, who graduate at the very top, earn the honor of the title "Surfman". There are only a hundred and fifty active-duty surfmen (about five of them women) among the five thousand boatswain's mates in the USCG.

These boat drivers are the very elite.

Who better to meet and see what happens than a rather lost radio broadcaster, filling in on his aunt's show, *Crossing the Bar.*

(Just a word of warning: the website I mentioned in the story, maritimetraffic.com, is a total *time suck.)*

1

"THIS IS CARLOS TORRES AND YOU'RE LISTENING TO *Crossing the Bar* where I bring you the latest news of what ships are crossing the Columbia River Bar. Today I also have on the radio the newest Surfman of the US Coast Guard search-and-rescue team stationed nearby at Cape D, that's Cape Disappointment, Washington. Actually, she's the newest Surf*woman*. But first, here's what ships are crossing the bar today."

Carlos sat in the small, circular tower that had always been the home of *Crossing the Bar*. His aunt had started it as a lark when she was between jobs, doing what she could to learn more about the ships she could watch entering the Columbia River from the window of her Astoria, Oregon late-Victorian home. Her podcast became an overnight phenomenon. At her listeners' request, she began learning what the ships were carrying in their holds. She then added in their last port of call, their owners, and even tidbits of their history—like just how many different flags they'd sailed under.

When she added interviews her podcast had changed from a local success to become the second most popular shipping news show anywhere in the world, coming in second only to the BBC's historic 150-year-old *Shipping Forecast.*

For months she'd been teasing him about taking over the show before she "withered at the microphone." As if. Women like Aunt Roz lived forever—at least he hoped so. When he'd finally confessed to a little interest—she'd instantly flown to Japan and booked a three-week passage on a car carrier running a load of Subarus from Japan back to Portland, Oregon, her idea of a fun vacation—and left the show to him to try out.

If it *had* been his idea, he'd probably have called the show *The Graveyard of the Pacific.* Over two thousand wrecks littered the sea floor around the Columbia Bar— the massive undersea sandbars churning gigantic surf even on the quietest days. It was generally acknowledged as the most dangerous shipping waters in the world.

But it wasn't his show, so he'd focus on doing Aunt Roz's version. He'd sat here beside her enough times as a teen to know the drill, often gathering the data from the various sites for her: The Kiro, *built in 1987 in the Yokohama, Japan yards, easily identified by the mismatched patch of blue paint on her starboard bow from her collision with a bridge abutment last fall—fault of a drunken captain, not a broken ship—currently underway from Shanghai with 4,432 TEU of containers of consumer products.*

A TEU was short for a Twenty-foot Equivalent Unit shipping container. As forty-footer lengths were far more standard, it was a good information tidbit to throw in that the ship was actually most likely carrying 2,216 forty-foot containers—which was a mind-boggling amount of "stuff." It was firmly in the Panamax class of ships that could fit through the original Panama Canal locks carrying up to 5,000 TEU. There was a larger class, the Neopanamax class, that could pass through the upgraded Canal locks with 14,000 TEU. Each time one of those loomed over the Columbia Bar, Carlos could only marvel at what was possible.

The Penny, *built...*

Using the MaritimeTraffic.com site, it was easy to see who was inbound and outbound—anyone could who cared. It was the stories behind the ships that kept the podcast so interesting. It's what had originally hooked him. He remembered one poor ship his "Auntie Roz" had reported on that had been pirated four separate times in a single passage. In Indonesia, there'd been a smash-and-grab job clearing out the crew's meager belongings. The second and third—while headed through the South China Sea—they'd had a quarter of their fuel oil siphoned off onto smaller, faster ships in hundred-thousand-gallon thefts. And the fourth pirating off Saipan had actually lasted three days before the pirates had become bored and simply left.

And yet the crews went to sea—a long and lonely life mostly seeking the money to send home to their families who they so rarely saw. Auntie Roz's podcast had given this backbone of international trade a face, at least across the Columbia Bar.

He continued reading down the traffic list.

2

"THAT'S THE SHIPPING THAT'S EXPECTED TO BE *CROSSING the Bar* today. Next, in my interview—"

Petty Officer Sarah Goodwin decided that the show host had a good voice, easy to listen to. She and Senior Chief Petty Officer McAllister had been sitting in the Cape D Guard station's communications room, listening to the shipping report and generally slagging each other.

"—we'll be talking to one of the newest of a very rare breed. The USCG Surfmen are the search-and-rescue experts at dozens of US ports."

The Senior Chief had been chapping her ass all morning about Sarah's pending interview on *Crossing the Bar.* That he was the one who'd tagged it onto her duty roster for the day hadn't bothered him. Not even a little. His final instruction to "play nice" with the podcaster they both knew was a complete waste of breath.

Three older brother Coasties and a Coastie mom? Plus her career as a one-out-of-five woman in the service hadn't taught her a thing about "nice." Mom had been through the Guard when she was more like one-in-twenty and had always told Sarah that being twice as hard-ass as any male was the only way to sail.

"And now I'd like to introduce you to the Coast Guard's newest surfwoman—"

She managed to get in the last word on the Senior Chief about playing nice.

"Seriously, Senior Chief?" Then flipped her own microphone live.

"—Petty Officer Sarah Goodwin. Hello, Sarah."

"Hey, Carlos. Thanks for having me on your 'cast," she offered in her sweetest voice while smiling at McAllister. "And it's Surfman. Just because a guy stows extra gear between his legs, doesn't mean he gets the title and I don't. We both had to pass through the same school to earn it."

McAllister rolled his eyes at her. If the man ever slouched, he'd have slouched in the chair in front of the console with utter resignation. Perfect.

She gave him the finger which earned her a smile. Any school with someone like "Mac" McAllister as an instructor made her damn proud to simply have survived, never mind passed.

"Surf*man* Sarah," the podcaster acknowledged without a stumble. Give him a point for that. "Or are you going to be updating the Coast Guard service so that all the guys will be called Surfwomen as well?"

And just that fast she went cold despite the warm office on the temperate September day. Actors versus Actresses. Heroes versus heroines. Waitresses. Stewardesses. That had been the world Mom had fought so hard against. Sarah was so damn sick of it. Her big brothers had been relentless on pushing that button, which had only made her dig in harder. Most of her hand-to-hand combat skills hadn't come from Coast Guard boot camp—they'd come from brawling with her brothers. Now they were scattered across the country by their different posts in the Guard, which was just as well.

McAllister must have seen something in her face, because his look went serious and he tapped his ear to remind her that she was on a live podcast. *Crossing the Bar* had a daily following in the tens of thousands and had always been supportive of the Coast Guard.

She managed to suppress the growl, but not the tone as she replied to Mr. Jerk Carlos Torres. "I'd never expect the men to meet the high standard such a title would require."

"And what would those extra qualifications be, Surf*man* Sarah?" Torres didn't have a clue how close he was to dying on the air. "Must be something pretty amazing. After all, it *is* an amazing list of skills to make Surfman, isn't it?"

It was. She found herself answering him out of habit —so many people didn't know about the training so she'd had lots of practice—explaining just what it took to get here. The familiar litany brought her back from the edge.

Join up, boot camp, Seaman, boat operations...

Somewhere along the way make Petty Officer Third Class. Schools. Choosing your rating.

Boatswain's Mate.

Lots more schools. And a serious amount of time doing "striker" on-the-job training. One of the proudest days of her life had been achieving her BM1—Boatswain's Mate 1st Class.

"No one outside the 'wet' military really understands what that means. The BM rating means that you have to know everything from winching strength on a cable to a crewman's capabilities, weather, sea, boats—the list goes on. Then you add to that. By becoming a coxswain, it doesn't just mean that you steer the boat. When the weather is busting sixty knots and breaking-wave-hell twenty meters over some poor sucker's head, it's your call on how to save them."

"And you're now passed or certified or whatever to do all that?" She became aware that the interviewer had been coaxing her along, feeding her questions. When had he taken control and she lost it?

McAllister was gone—apparently deciding she wasn't about to disgrace the Guard. Fool.

"Yes. That's what being awarded a Surfman Badge means."

The interviewer gave a low whistle of surprise that almost sounded impressed. "Damn, woman."

And there it was again. There had to be a way that she could whup that out of at least one male's head.

Then she had an idea.

A nasty idea.

It *definitely* wouldn't involve playing nice.

3

CARLOS GLANCED UP AT THE SKY AND DECIDED THAT HE shouldn't be in too much trouble. September in the Pacific Northwest was changeable in mood, but tended toward the more pleasant. It wasn't until October that the weather really flipped. Today was sixty degrees and maybe fifteen miles-an-hour of wind—thirteenish knots he corrected himself. Sailors always thought in nautical miles for reasons passing understanding.

Then he looked down at the dock again and was less sure. The weather here at the Cape Disappointment Coast Guard station in Ilwaco, Washington on the far bank of the wide Columbia River was blowing up stormy right from the gate.

A Senior Chief Petty Officer McAllister, with the sense of humor of a lead brick, had come to fetch him from security.

"Always glad to have a visit from *Crossing the Bar*," he grumbled a greeting. "Of course your aunt never went out of her way to antagonize my best new Surfman."

Carlos opened his mouth...

McAllister looked *really* unhappy about something.

...so Carlos closed his mouth again.

He'd thought that he and Surf*man* Sarah Goodwin were just having a little friendly banter for the show. In fact, they'd gone on long enough that he'd had to end the show and just keep recording. He'd briefly muted his own connection to Surfman Sarah to promise the podcast listeners that he'd be continuing the interview in future episodes. He'd gotten enough material to make it a five-part series.

Then at the end of the interview, Petty Officer Sarah Goodwin BM1 had asked if he'd like to go out on a training cruise the next day. He knew that Aunt Roz got out on the cargo ships whenever she could. If he was ever going to be serious about taking over the show, he figured he'd have to do the same. And on his first day she'd offered him the chance to try it out.

Also, as a one-up on his aunt, she'd never gone out on the search-and-rescue surf boats. She'd been out with the bar pilots' transport tugs as they motored out to vessels to guide them back over the bar. She'd also had a local helo pilot who exchanged free sightseeing ads on the show for giving her a quick ride out onto the occasional incoming vessel.

But to get out on the working craft of the US Coast Guard, the 47-foot Motor Lifeboat, better known as the 47-MLB, that was a definite coup. He'd planned on getting major mileage out of that at the next family dinner.

Or so he'd thought as he blithely accepted Surfman Sarah's offer.

Aunt Roz's and Dad's brother had been a US Coast Guard helicopter mechanic for thirty years here by the Columbia—still was. And three of his four daughters had married Coasties. (The fourth, Maggie, a total reprobate and the most fun of the lot, had become a helicopter mechanic for a group of firefighters and married one of the team's civilian helo pilots. Total outcast at family gatherings. He hung with her whenever he could.) But what with all the brothers-in-law's training, he knew how to read a ticked-off Coastie.

And when that Coastie was a Senior Chief Petty Officer, Carlos knew the wind was going to be blowing cold no matter what the weather.

The Senior Chief turned to look at him.

Carlos didn't recall coming to a stop at the head of the pier.

"Go on down, boy. Last boat in the line. You *earned* it." This time the Senior's grimace might have been a mocking smile. He slapped Carlos hard enough on the shoulder that it was a miracle he wasn't catapulted out to sea as some part of a Man Overboard (and don't bother rescuing him) Drill. He and the Senior were the same height, and Carlos liked keeping fit, but he had nothing on the man for raw power.

Turning the slam's momentum into a forward stumble, he headed down the pier. There were five of the boats tied up: two to the left, then three to the right—all parked stern-in along narrow floating docks. Another group of three more were moored on another leg of the long pier. Each crew he passed looked down at him from their boats and then made some snide comment he could never quite hear. But he heard the laughter trailing behind him.

The long path of shame.

It was like the long walk to the principal's office, one he'd worn well over the years. "Directionless." "Inattentive." "Joker." (Prankster actually, but he tried not to correct Dr. Bream too often. Pointing out during his first visit with the man that he'd been named for a fish—but a pretty one, good eating too—hadn't earned him as much good will as you might think.) He'd pulled any number of stunts over the years: reprogramming the school bells to ring at odd times and changing out the recording of the national anthem for morning announcements with *Louie Louie* by the Notre Dame Marching Band—the best version in his humble opinion.

Carlos managed to get As when he cared: English, History, Journalism. Cs when he didn't: just about everything else except track-and-field. No college. He'd wanted to get a little "down and dirty." Which had turned out to be less fun than it sounded over the last five years. He'd done some paid blogging, a little sports writing, local cable TV, made it to the news desk. And got bored out of his gourd.

A local broadcast station—a good local in Seattle—offered him a test at a weekend anchor slot.

We think you've got what it takes. We want you to bring it to our market.

He sat in as a "guest co-anchor" for a pair of evening and late-night news slots.

He'd quit the cable station the next day. But instead of turning his car north for Seattle, he'd turned west and ended up in Aunt Roz's Victorian-tower broadcast studio. Quite how or why that had happened still eluded him.

And high school. It had been a long time since Carlos had thought about that long walk down the echoing concrete hallway between all the sports trophies he'd helped win and all the academic awards that he hadn't.

"Shake it off, dude." Though he kept his voice low as another round of titters followed him along. "Yeah, just keep that up, guys. Who knew that full-grown Coasties 'tittered'? Definitely going into the next podcast." He felt better for that decision.

The last boat down the line didn't have a tittering crew watching him go by. They were busy preparing to go to sea.

A pair of guys in full float gear were checking over their equipment. They were dressed in bright red, head-to-toe float suits with the hoods tugged back. Another guy with a clipboard and a toolbelt was conferring with them.

And up on the open bridge, there was a woman standing there like she was a Greek goddess. At least that was his first impression. The sun, still low to the east, was dazzling behind her. She had her feet planted wide and her arms crossed in front of her. She rolled so easily with the rocking of the boat that it seemed she was the one who stayed still and the rest of the world bobbed and dipped around her center. He couldn't see anything else about her because she also wore one of the bulky float suits. Maybe her hair was made of purest gold, maybe that was just the sun—it was hard to tell.

"Mr. Torres. So glad you could join us." Just like on the radio, Petty Office Sarah Goodwin had a low, warm voice that sounded deceptively friendly. In fact, if not for the Senior Chief's warning, he'd have thought it was. Now he could hear the chill sweeping south from Alaska. Or perhaps the Arctic Ocean. Deep chill. He wasn't just in the deep end of the pool; the bottom had gone missing while he wasn't watching.

The 47-MLB was just that, forty-seven feet of custom-designed purebred Motor Lifeboat. He'd done what research he could last night. It was all aluminum. No air-filled bladders that made the smaller 42-foot Near Shore Lifeboat look like a Zodiac on steroids with rubber-bladder sides. Five feet of length was only the smallest of the differences. The 47-MLB had an open bridge exposed to the weather and an enclosed bridge that stayed watertight even if the boat became fully submerged. There was even a watertight survivor compartment complete with medical gear and a stretcher if they had to do a helicopter evacuation. Twin Detroit diesel engines could practically make the boat fly.

It was forty-seven feet, eighteen tons (incredibly light for a boat of this size), and over a million dollars of mean, robust, Coast Guard machine.

"Thanks for having me." If she was going to pretend to play it light, so could he.

She watched him for a long moment, then shrugged.

"Vicks and Marnham. Get him suited up to get wet. You don't mind getting wet, do you?"

"No, ma'am," seemed the safest answer. But he risked adding, "Though usually I'm more of a track-and-field guy." Because why the hell not?

4

SARAH MANAGED TO KEEP THE SMILE OFF HER FACE UNTIL she was turned away. The float crew would get him in a suit while she finished checking over the pre-mission list.

Javits came over with his engineer's sign-off that all of his systems were good to go and she sent him to suit up as well.

Track and field.

He had the shape for it. At first she'd thought it was a swimmer's form, all lean except for legs and shoulders. That how you knew a true rescue swimmer. Most swimmers built up the big shoulders, but the real top guys—like Vicks and Marnham—had thighs of steel as well.

Mr. Torres had surprised her. She'd expected a mouse of a man who never crawled out from his mom's basement except to get his delivery pizza. Six foot of strapping Latino with dark curly hair, olive skin, and a bright smile just didn't fit her mental image. Neither did track-and-field. He was built for it with a top-swimmer's legs filling out his jeans. Though while his shoulders were good, they weren't quite broad enough to be a USCG swimmer.

That's what almost made her laugh in his face. How many times had Senior Chief McAllister lambasted her over these last months about making assumptions?

"Every situation is an unknown. Even if you know it, it's an unknown. Next time you bump up against a log, it's going to be a WWII floating mine with your name carved in the rust. Next time you pull up to help a dismasted sailboat, it's going to be the conning tower of a narco-submarine and they're going to come out guns blazing to take your boat. You gonna give it to them, Goodwin?"

"Never, Senior Chief!" she'd shout from full attention.

And then he'd set her another scenario and she'd walk straight into his next trap.

She rubbed her fingers over her Surfman badge: crossed oars over a life preserver. Only a hundred and sixty active-duty men and women wore these. They were the smallest specialty in the entire Coast Guard and the feeling was still shiny and new. No miscreant radio jockey was going to make her feel one bit less than she was.

Carlos Torres was handsome and fit rather than basement-pizza pale. *Fine.* She'd see just how wet he could take.

"Hi." He'd come up beside her without her even noticing. That was bad; usually she could feel a seagull even thinking about landing on the aft rail of her boat.

"You ready for this?" She wanted to keep him in his place. His dark eyes were dead-level with her own. She scared off a lot of men with her height, but it didn't seem to bother him. He looked damn good in a float suit.

"Always," he replied with that naive ease of the unsuspecting.

"Sit your ass over there," she aimed a finger at the port-side chair. He was in her world now and there was no listening audience to make her pretend to be nice. "Put on the seat belt. You do not take it off without a direct order from me. And if you touch a single control or lever, I will take your belt off myself and throw you overboard. Are we clear?"

"Yes, ma'am." He shot her a salute that said he'd never served. But it was close enough to right that it meant he'd watched too many war movies or something. Also, his smile just grew bigger as if he knew he was pissing her off and was enjoying himself.

She glanced down at the morning's surf report on her own console and made a bet with herself on just how long he wasn't going to keep wearing that smile.

5

"Cushy," Carlos dropped into the chair. "How hard is the ride on this boat?"

Sarah looked over at him with narrowed eyes. Blue eyes that seemed to see everything and true blonde hair just long enough to make a short ponytail. BM Goodwin might sound like a force of nature, but she looked, oddly, like a fighter. It wasn't that she wasn't beautiful, because... well, *damn*. It was that there was a determined set to her expression that he bet could run over anything in her way: man, rough surf, or Neopanamax container ship. He wondered how many times *she'd* tracked the long path down to the principal's office during her high school years. More than a few.

"Why the surprise?" Carlos enjoyed doing that to her.

"Most civilians think the seat is cushy for its own sake."

"Uh-huh. Where you from?"

"Chicago originally."

"Great Lakes. That's heavy duty," Carlos was impressed.

Sarah looked surprised that he knew that as well. Most people didn't even know the Coast Guard also guarded those inland waters among many others. The Great Lakes boasted sixteen Coast Guard stations between ship and air stations—the entire Mississippi River system only boasted four stations. The storms thrown up on the Great Lakes had actually claimed far more ships than the Columbia Bar. Of course they were also far more expansive. Still, she definitely knew about the wind-water dynamic that so many landlubbers didn't understand.

"I grew up local," he explained. "And while I was never crazy enough to surf this section of the Oregon Coast—which requires a wetsuit and no fear of imminent death—I've been out in the chop when it starts blowing a gale with no warning. Most locals don't even get interested in a storm around here until it crosses fifty knots. And it isn't until it gets up into the eighties that we consider trekking out in our pickups to the headlands and watch the thirty-foot surf rolling in under the horizontal rain. I've never been out in a motor lifeboat, but I'm not dumb enough to think this padding is for comfort."

It earned him a grunt of acknowledgement. Then she turned her attention to casting off lines and getting underway.

He noticed that she didn't snap and bark at the crew for all of her unexpected attitude. They all moved with the calm efficiency of an integrated team. That was part of the reason he'd ended up in track-and-field—he sucked at "team." He could do his part of a relay just fine, by treating it as an individual challenge to outperform not only the other teams, but the other members of his own as well. Sarah's team might have all been cogs of the same wheel they were so smooth.

She worked the heavy aluminum steering wheel with one hand and the pair of red-knobbed throttles with the other as if they were extensions of her body. He also noticed that she too wore her seatbelt, meaning she didn't just make him wear his to keep him out of trouble.

Just how rough a ride *had* he agreed to?

Inspecting his own station, he didn't have a wheel. One arm of the chair had a small lever at the end marked "Port" and "Starboard"—steering adjustments if someone had to work from his seat instead of the one with the wheel. He also had a matching pair of the red throttle levers. Carlos made a special note to not even think about bumping any of them. There were engine-speed and rudder-angle indicators, engine start and stop buttons, and not much else. Mounted between their two positions were radar and radios.

In front of her was another radio and some more electronics, but less than he'd expected. The more he looked, the more he realized that it wasn't about someone tending an amazing machine. A 47-MLB was a simple, seaworthy tool used by a capable woman for going to the rescue.

"Superwoman!" The exclamation was just knocked out of him as the boat slipped out from where the Coast

Guard station lay tucked behind Ruby Island and headed into the throat of the Columbia River.

Sarah glared at him. He had about enough of her silent, feminist-action shit.

"Tough, lady. If the superhero uniform fits, wear it."

IF CARLOS TORRES WAS BUSY PICTURING HER IN SOME skintight superhero outfit, she wasn't going to drown him —she was going to gut him like a salmon.

Assumptions, Goodwin. She could hear McAllister even over the roar of the two Detroit diesels as she took them up on the planing hull to twenty-two knots and headed toward the open ocean.

"What's your problem, Torres?" Sarah shouted over to him.

"My problem?" He wasn't clutching the chair arms like some desperate civilian as they began popping over the two-meter waves washing in from the sea. Instead he sat with his hands folded in his lap as calm as could be. "I got no problems. Sunny day. Out for the morning on a 47-MLB with a beautiful and skilled woman who wants to jettison me overboard every time I pay her a compliment. What's up with that anyway?"

"Nothing's up with that," she clenched her jaw and faced the sea.

Directly starboard lay the tip of the half-mile long North Jetty that ran out from Cape D, Washington. It anchored at the end of Peacock Spit, which had probably claimed more shipwrecks than anywhere else in the world over the last two hundred years. Two miles to port lay the tip of the three-mile long South Jetty stretching out from Clatsop Spit at the very top corner of Oregon. In between lay her job.

She scanned the area as they bounced along the wavetops. Five cruisers under fifty feet, agile enough to be doing pretty much whatever they damn well pleased —which created headaches for everyone, accounting for over twenty percent of Coast Guard rescues every season. A twenty-six-foot daysailer tacking neatly across shipping lanes in a gap between passing ships and not looking to be stupid enough to be headed out to sea over the bar. Two inbound container ships and an outbound bulk carrier all showing their transponders on her radar sweep—meant that three of the sixteen bar pilots were working this morning. Everything appeared in order.

"So, you treat compliments as insults out of some sort of self-defense mechanism. That's interesting."

"I thought you were a journalist not a headshrinker."

"Me? No, I'm neither. Just a directionless bum with a radio show for three weeks while Aunt Roz is on vacation."

"And you're fine with that?"

"Why shouldn't I be?"

Because it makes you even lamer to admit it than being a directionless bum in the first place.

"Personally, I've always found overachieving to be a waste of energy."

"So, what *do* you find worthwhile?" She'd thought to run some shore patrols along the South Jetty, but rejected that. She wanted this Carlos Torres to hurt a little. So instead, she swung wide of the North Jetty and turned northwest for the heavy surf off the Peacock Spit.

Javits must have read her mind, because he came up on the bridge with a pair of safety harnesses. He used one to latch Mr. Bum Torres' suit to a safety ring on the bridge so that he was doubly attached to the boat.

Normally her engineer would be in the seat occupied by Torres. Instead, he harnessed into one of the jump seats directly behind his usual position. Nicer than she'd have been, but then Javits was a nice guy.

Vicks and Marnham would be sitting in the Survivor Compartment, belted in and probably playing a game of Gin Rummy. How had they become blasé about getting out on the water? Every single time she escaped the dock was like the first time she'd gone to a rock concert—some part of her disconnected and danced. She'd always been the perfect student: straight As, head of the volleyball team with her height, and anchor on the swim relay team. And she could count the number of kids she was in touch with from high school on a closed fist.

Why had wanting to be best been such a crime?

It wasn't a crime in the Coast Guard. It had value.

Even Vicks and Marnham, with their ever-so-chill game of Rummy, were actually top flight—they just made a whole point pretending they were too cool to care. They were already top-rated swimmers and she knew they spent most of their off hours preparing for the brutal USCG rescue swimmer course—a 24-week challenge with an eighty percent failure rate. They were so good that even McAllister was giving them better than even odds of making it.

She never fraternized inside the Guard. And she'd yet to find a worthwhile man outside the Guard. Good thing she was used to being alone.

Sarah checked the surf ahead. The bright sun glared off the breaking crests, but added little warmth. Temperatures ran a consistent five to ten degrees lower out on the ocean here, especially when the offshore fog banks were nudging shoreward.

A pair of 47-MLBs were "in it" farther up the line—a new Surfman class getting their "scare them off the boat" ride. First day of class, driven straight into the heaviest surf. There were always a couple that decided they were in over their heads and bailed. Even some heavy-weather-certified coxswains bailed after a day in the Cape D surf.

The trick was, the waves always looked milder than they were. From the east, the Columbia pumped a quarter of a million cubic feet per second into the ocean —the fifth largest river by discharge in North America and thirty-eighth in the world. From the south, a northbound sea current traveled up the coast at a couple kilometers per hour. And from the west, or any direction the Pacific Ocean was in the mood for, sea swells that had been building energy across ten thousand kilometers ran into the other two currents and created utter mayhem just where the ships needed to go. When the tide was outbound and the swells were inbound, like this morning, everything doubled up.

She shared a glance with Javits.

He nodded that everything and everyone was ready—which meant he'd already warned the float guys they were headed into the rough. He included a grimace that said she was pushing it.

When she shrugged a reply that maybe she was, he waved her toward the waves. There was a reason she liked this crew. She knew if she rolled them sideways onto their beam's end, the float guys would simply slap a hand down on their Rummy cards until she righted.

Sarah took the first big wave at a sixty-degree angle, goosing the starboard engine hard as the bow lifted up the face. Ten meters of breaking waves slapped the 47-MLB solidly on the butt, slamming her straight as Sarah shot up over the top.

Half the hull went airborne before they tipped and the nose slammed down on the back of the wave. Just like she'd planned.

She heard Torres grunt with the impact as she was judging the next wave. Her obvious move would take her closer to the two boats giving the First Day cruise, which the instructors wouldn't appreciate. Instead, she let the next wave break hard across the deck.

"Take a breath," she shouted to Torres moments before it hit. Which, like walking into one of McAllister's traps, left her with no air of her own while the 47-MLB lay on its side and a couple tons of sea spray robbed them of air. She was the one sputtering by the time they hit clear air.

She cranked the wheel hard and took the next wave— a chaotic slasher from the south—head-on with a burst of diesel power.

Unlike the older 42-MLB that plowed through the waves, the 47 climbed like the champion it was and shot over the top with almost no water on the deck.

All three of them grunted in unison as the bow slammed down and she began carving for the next wave. She needed to check if Torres had hit his limit yet. Scaring a civilian was one thing, terrifying a radio personality was something McAllister wouldn't appreciate. But the last wave had tossed her toward the First Dayers again and she had to concentrate on hitting the next wave at the same angle they did so that all three boats kept their spacing along the wave face.

"Is this pretty typical?" Torres shouted out to her. He didn't sound upset. Instead he was curious.

"Pretty mild for Peacock Point," she shouted back, too busy to say more as she watched Chief Wester on the next boat to see what his next line of attack would be.

"This is about half of what the boat is rated to take," Javits answered for her. He was the boat's mechanic and always thought of everything from that angle. "Of course to us—"

They all held their breaths as a wall of spray slashed over them and she was able to angle away from the other two boats.

"—as passengers, when we're getting up into the kind

of violence this boat can still handle, it will feel about ten times worse."

This time she could feel Torres watching her.

She took advantage of a bad break to the south, to let the next wave slam Torres from behind without warning.

His sputters when they resurfaced were very gratifying.

7

CARLOS WOULD HAVE LAUGHED IF HE HAD ANY AIR.
Surfman Sarah Goodwin was definitely out to get him.
He'd have to watch himself around her.

He tried to imagine "ten times worse" and decided
that he was glad it wouldn't be him feeling it. He'd
already bottomed out the chair's heavy padding twice
with breath-stealing butt plants. At first he'd felt insulted
at Javits doubling Carlos' harness; now he was grateful. It
was very comforting to feel firmly attached to the boat
when the waves tossed eighteen tons of aluminum and
five humans about like a bath toy.

He tried to watch what Sarah was looking for as she
surveyed the next wave and drove them into it, but she
was too distracting. Her focus, her whole being, had such
a clear purpose. Her, the boat, the wave. Tweak a throttle,
cock the wheel, brace for the blow, already turning for
the next while the boat still shuddered from the hit. Scan
right and left. Other waves? Other craft?

No chance to ask as they plunged back into the roiling

mess that was the sea. Waves seemed to come from every direction, yet still she took them one after another. One moment he had a high view out to sea and back to the beach. The next they plunged into a trough where the entire vista was made up of a bowl of wind-shredded water.

After twenty crestings, or maybe twice that, he decided that the two other boats had left when he wasn't paying attention to them. And still Sarah took on the waves.

He wondered if she was even aware of the passage of time.

Not Superwoman, he decided. More like some daughter of Poseidon, Greek God of the Sea.

Maybe she was—

"Help! Somebody help us!" Squawked over the radio in a shrill scream that broke up even as they transmitted. "Please! Can any...hear...? Help!"

"My hands are a little full," Sarah shouted above the roar of the surf and engines, somehow calmly, and nodded toward the two microphones hanging from the center console. "Take the left one and don't say a single word I don't tell you."

He grabbed it, and forgot to hold his breath as the next wave slammed over them. He surfaced coughing seawater out of his lungs.

"Real smooth, Torres."

He nearly strangled himself suppressing the next choking hack.

"Okay, start: This is the US Coast Guard. Please identify."

Carlos held the key to transmit and echoed her words.

"Oh thank God. This is Tom. No one's been answering!"

He shared a smile with Sarah. Damn but the woman had an amazing smile. Made him wonder just how rarely she let it out to play. It shifted her from stern to whimsical in a single flash of brightness.

"Hi, Tom," he echoed Sarah as she drove hard to the south back toward the main mouth of the river. The waves were so rough, he couldn't sight land, but the sun was to the south and it was blinding him at the moment. "What's the problem and where are you?"

"We were trying. To enter the Columbia. Got swept past it. Big waves! Like nothing I've ever seen! Now they're worse— Shit!"

The last word was Carlos' own.

He shot out an arm as Sarah scowled at him. Just off the starboard side of the 47-MLB, the prow of a sailboat shot out of a wave—not over the top, but straight out of the center of a towering wave face.

It was aimed straight for the back of Sarah's head.

He grabbed her shoulder and hauled her down until her head was practically in his lap. It would have been if her seatbelt hadn't been pulled so tight.

The white V of fiberglass crunched into the stout railing close by her right arm. It slid back along the rail, slamming into one of the uprights supporting the radar mast, then the prow fell astern. The boat rolled in the waves. Tumbling sideways, he briefly saw the keel as it rolled completely over.

Sarah was sitting up and he tried to give a helpful shove.

Her hands were slamming the controls even as she moved.

"Deep breath!" She shouted. "We'll right in twelve seconds."

Carlos gasped in deeply and wondered what she meant, just as he felt the next roller slam into him from behind. The sailboat had knocked them beam-on to the biggest wave he'd seen yet.

All sense of direction disappeared. Gravity was doing one thing. His float suit was doing another with its buoyancy. And his gut was doing a third as the seatbelt yanked him along with the boat's roll.

The pressure built as the water did its best to rip him bodily out of his seat.

This wasn't spray.

He was completely submerged in "green" water—the solid wall of true ocean.

Blinking against the saltwater made it feel as if his eyeballs were being ripped from his head. The pressure built against his eardrums.

Sarah had shouted something other than to take a breath.

Twelve seconds.

It had already been minutes. He could feel the pressure squeezing his chest, telling him to breathe. He wanted to claw at his seatbelt to free himself, but remembered the second harness. No idea how it had attached.

By an act of pure will, he began counting backwards

from twelve and picturing the long hall of the school's meaningless trophy display.

Twelve, the debate club.

Eleven, the math team on the right.

These were going to be the last images of his life?

Ten, basketball on the left.

Really? Pathetic!

Nine, the cheer squad of all ridiculous things (the school's only state-level competitor other than his own track-and-field All-State that year).

He needed to get a different life next time.

Eight, the yearbook club.

Like that was something he cared about.

Seven, *The Feed,* the online school news forum he'd run for two years had won a statewide broadcasting award.

Six—

He slammed back into the air as the boat completed its roll, tipping far enough over the other way that he gasped in a fresh breath in prep for going under again. They mostly righted so he didn't need it.

"Still with us, Tom?" Somehow he'd held onto the microphone and managed to echo Sarah's words.

The silence was ominous as he scanned around looking for the sailboat. They didn't always right themselves the way the MLB was designed to.

"There," Sarah was already turning for it as another wave tumbled it upright. No mast. That's why Tom hadn't been able to reach anyone. Losing his mast, he'd lost his antenna. The only reason they'd heard him was they were so close they were getting the bleed directly off his transmitter.

Glancing back, Carlos saw that somehow the two members of the float team had managed to get onto the rear deck and were moving confidently along it. He noted they each had a safety harness with two clips, one of which was always attached somewhere on the boat.

He tried Tom again, with no luck.

He twisted to look at Javits in the seat behind his, to see if he needed Carlos to do something. No Javits.

Before Carlos could panic, he spotted him on the afterdeck. Somehow he'd negotiated down a five-step ladder while they were being tumbled about. Even as Carlos watched, Javits began pulling two-inch yellow polypropylene line off one of the two big drums mounted there.

In moments, Vicks was in the water. Marnham was paying out a line attached to Vick's harness as the man swam toward the leaping sailboat while dragging the two-inch line with him.

Somehow, in the impossible surf, Sarah had gotten them lined up stern-first in front of the sailboat. Each time a wave battered them, the swimmer resurfaced somewhere closer to the sailboat.

The next time the sailboat's bow dug into the face of a wave, Vicks rode the wave crest above it—his arms moving like pinwheels in a hurricane. Then he was lifted out of the water as the bow emerged sluggishly from beneath him. In moments, he had the yellow line tied off on the bow's anchor cleat. Then he began moving aft.

"Tom?" Carlos tried the radio again as Sarah added power to the engines.

"...insid... Think we capsiz..."

"Tom. Listen, there is a Coast Guard swimmer on your boat. Move to the rear, but do not try to exit the cabin until he reaches you."

"O..ay."

A wave swept the sailboat end to end. Vicks rode it like a surfer down the length of the deck, then managed to catch himself on a lifeline stanchion before he was swept overboard.

"That boat isn't long for the world," he shouted at Sarah. It was wallowing lower with each inundation.

8

REGRETTABLY CARLOS' ASSESSMENT MATCHED HERS.

She'd hoped to drag them out into calmer water, then remembered the forecast. Surf building through the morning. There'd been a storm somewhere out at sea and the ocean swell had kept moving even without the storm pushing at it any longer.

The rougher water had been teaching her its own lessons this morning. It was a rare opportunity to learn and she'd concentrated on studying the interplay of the truly big surf. McAllister had told her stories of what waves could do—and her long stretch at the National Motor Lifeboat School had taught her a lot. But today had been running rougher even than usual for Peacock Spit, so now she had the images and the body memory to attach to McAllister's tales.

Until the sailboat tried to kill her.

Capsized, dismasted, she still should have seen it.

Somehow.

Carlos had. When it counted, he'd kept his head as well as any Guardsman and that was an unexpected gift. He'd also saved her at least a bad battering.

A quick glance showed that tops of the waves were tearing off spindrifts of spray. No longer merely rough surf—the wind had blown up a fresh gale of forty knots while she'd been working the boat. She grabbed the other mic that would connect her to the Coast Guard station.

"This is MLB 562 in tow with a dismasted Cal 39 sailboat three miles due west of Peacock Spit. Forecast?"

"Blowing forty, climbing to fifty over the next hour. Seas your location twelve meters, expecting fast build to fifteen-plus. Do you require assistance?"

"Swimmer on a line aboard the Cal 39. Effecting rescue of one crew…"

Carlos flashed two fingers, then waggled the hand in doubt as he raised a third.

She thought about it. Tom *had* kept referring to "we."

Sarah spun the wheel to take the next wave on the starboard quarter.

"…possibly two or more. Helo aloft in case we need eyes. Cal 39 will be gone under before second MLB could arrive. Out." She hung up the microphone.

"What's my status, Carlos?" She couldn't afford to look away from the waves. The MLB could function effectively to sixty knots of wind and twenty-meter waves, but doing a rescue in those conditions was right out at the limits.

"You've got about fifty feet of tow line to the Cal

which has barely a foot of freeboard now. Vicks has gone into the cabin which must be mostly flooded."

She calculated the time to haul two civilians across the gap separating the boats as she ducked under a major breaker that actually slapped the MLB's bow under the water rather than letting it ride over. Getting under the curl of a breaking wave was always a bad idea.

But her baby rode it out—splitting the wave across the front of the bridge and only hitting them with spray. The MLB finally popped up like a cork with enough force to nearly cut Sarah in two with her seatbelt. They were all going to be black-and-blue after this one.

Carlos blew out a loud breath beside her, then glanced back.

"No boat. No boat. No boat... There! On the surface, awash."

Out of options, Sarah cut the power to both engines.

Then she turned and saw that the situation was just as bad as she imagined.

Drifting backwards, she used a small burst of starboard power to avoid ramming the sailboat's bow with her stern.

Javits was winding the line back onto the drum as fast as he could, but the drum was built for strength not speed.

"Prepare to cut," she shouted as loudly as she could. They were less than ten feet apart, but the roar of wind and water—she could only hope that he heard her.

They pulled parallel with the bow.

"Cut!" she yelled and continued drifting back. The 47-

MLB had a walkway along either side of the cabin. It ran from the aft deck to the foredeck, five feet above the water. But by flipping up a grating, a notch in the hull formed a recovery well that was just a foot above the water.

The others would know what she was doing.

She hoped.

Pulling alongside any craft in such rough seas was incredibly dangerous. Shifting across two or more injured civilians and a CG swimmer was a wild gamble at best, but she didn't have another play. If she ordered them all into the water, could the approaching helo even find them again in such turbulent wave conditions? Not likely. Not until they were corpses washed up on the vast sandy stretches of Long Beach to the north.

The training that had been driven straight into her instincts kept her concentrated on her part of the mission —looking down over the starboard side of her boat and trying to calculate how to keep it within a foot of the sinking sailboat as the waves slammed them about. The wind was from the port side—trying to topple her over on top of the sailboat—and it wasn't as if she had a bow thruster to hold herself in place sideways.

But the MLB would offer some wind and wave shield for the rescue, so she'd taken the upwind side. Which should work.

Hopefully.

She could feel Torres straining to see what was happening over her side of the boat.

"Do *not* unharness from your seat," she shouted at

him. "Keep watch to port and let me know if anything big is coming."

"Define big," he answered on a half-laugh, commenting on the biggest surf she'd certainly ever driven in. His laugh cut off in a choke as spray inundated them for a moment.

9

Sarah wasn't sure how she'd let herself get talked into this, but there was no backing out.

You owe me at least a beer for trying to kill me, Carlos had said at the dock as the ambulance took away Tom and his girlfriend (two broken wrists and a concussion between them).

In a fit of weakness, she'd agreed. She should have known he'd turn it into a beer and a pizza, which was far too much like a date.

Inferno Lounge.

Perfect, she was in hell.

Carlos had beat her there, because—of all stupid things—she'd vacillated on what to wear. Like her wardrobe held so many options. Jeans, a blouse, and a fleece vest, because Oregon evenings were always cool by definition. Then she'd had to double back for a windbreaker, because it was September. Then for her wallet because she was a basket case.

It would have been easy if it had just been dinner

with Carlos Torres from *Crossing the Bar*. He'd done a damned decent job of being an asset instead of a liability on the rescue.

It was much more complicated after she'd listened to his latest couple of podcasts. He'd interlaced her initial interview with his own observations about the Surfman training and then the rescue. It had been...riveting.

"Damn. You're hired, Goodwin." Senior Chief McAllister told her after they'd listened to it together.

"Didn't do anything unusual, Senior Chief."

"Not for you, maybe. Your request of station assignment better be on my desk in the morning and it better say Cape Disappointment in all three preference slots or you and I are going to have words, Missy. Search-and-rescue for now. Assistant Instructor as soon as a slot opens." Then he'd stomped off.

She'd *Missy* him a good one next chance she had.

But now she had to deal with the man who had just gotten the Coast Guard's National Motor Lifeboat School an international recognition. Carlos' story had been picked up by the major news feeds. The only way she'd protected herself was by declaring he had an exclusive on the story and routing all of the reporters' calls to *Crossing the Bar's* phone number.

"Hey Surf*woman*," Carlos rose to his feet as she approached the table.

"And the reason I'm not killing you for that?"

He smiled broadly, "Because you already proved my point."

"Which is?"

"You proved that Surf*woman* is indeed a superior standard that mere Surf*men* can only hope to live up to."

Sarah sighed and dropped into a seat across from him. The Inferno Lounge wasn't as hideous as the name. It was a comfortable old bar and restaurant out on the edge of the waterfront. Rather than taking a table in some dark corner, Carlos had chosen one up against the big sweep of glass. Just feet away lay the broad reach of the Columbia. The bridge between Astoria, Oregon and Ilwaco, Washington, arched against the deep orange and gold of the sunset sky. From here she could see all of the shipping moving through the mouth of the Columbia. He'd even sat so that her seat looked out to sea while his looked upriver, which was decent of him—she knew him well enough now to know that the thoughtfulness was intentional.

"You asked me a question," he said after they'd ordered beer and a loaded pizza.

"I...when? What was it?"

"You asked what I was, a headshrinker or a journalist? And I told you that I was just a directionless bum. You asked if I was okay with that."

"You said you were."

"I lied."

"Still doesn't tell me if you were a journalist or a headshrinker."

Carlos smiled at her. It was a strange smile. More as if he was smiling at himself.

"What?"

"You really want to know the answer?"

She shrugged a yes.

"My problem was," and he aimed those dark eyes of his at her. She suddenly couldn't look away. "That in that moment, I had just figured out that you and I graduated from school the same year. Made me feel like I hadn't done shit with my life. Hell of a depressing thought for a sunny day out on the ocean."

"No, you've—" He rested a warm hand on hers for a moment and silenced her.

"I said *was.*"

"Oh no. You're one of those Word People, aren't you?" Sarah couldn't suppress a groan. Her middle brother was that way, stopping the most normal conversation to clarify, rectify, prevaricate—whatever. "Words always have meaning and you have to use just the right one?"

"Guilty as charged. Professional journalist, amateur headshrinker."

Maybe she could like him despite that. Maybe not. She'd wait and see.

"Just a week before I met you, I got the golden job call. *Come be a news anchor at a major station.* It was weekend anchor, but it was a good slot. Real opportunity."

"But you're here."

"Yep," he sipped his beer after it arrived and looked out at a passing bulk carrier headed to Portland to onload soda ash. "And I didn't know why either. I'd gotten in the car headed to Seattle—and ended up in my aunt's driveway here in Astoria."

"You know why now?" She tasted her own beer, a local porter she hadn't known—not much reason to go get a pint when you weren't seeing anyone.

"I do." And he didn't explain.

"And?" Guessing games weren't her strength either.

He just pointed at her.

"What? You're suddenly in love with me?"

"No, that'll come later."

She opened her mouth, then closed it again so that she didn't choke on some random wave that might crash over her unexpectedly.

"You'll have to meet the family first. We're quite a local clan here. A lot of Coasties, a few firefighters," then he tapped himself on the chest, "and the new broadcaster of *Crossing the Bar.* Survive one of those family dinners, then we'll talk over the falling in love part."

Meeting his family? No way in hell was she meeting any lame-ass bum's— Except Carlos wasn't. Or was he? She didn't know what to think.

"I don't do what you do. But I realized that I do know how to tell others about that."

He certainly did. She was still breathless from hearing his recounting of the rescue, which had covered a mere twelve lines in her official report. That he saw her the way he did. Powerful and female. Competent, worthy, and desirable. All mixed together. All in one person she barely recognized.

Her mother had always delineated that you could either be a woman or a member of the military and that doing both wasn't possible. Not on the outside. And Sarah had taken that into the inside as well until she'd totally believed it.

Carlos was showing her that perhaps that wasn't true.

"And," Carlos continued. This time she could feel that

his smile was for her. "I'm especially good if it's
something I care about. I was raised here. My family is
here. Cousins, sisters, uncles, parents, Aunt Roz, all of
them. Thanks to you, I know that I came back here rather
than going to Seattle because I care about *this* place. I
care about *these* people." He waved a hand at the
shipping channel so nearby, now shadowed in the
evening light.

It was a breathtaking statement. Sarah's family was...
scattered. Rarely coming together because they were a
Coastie family and one person's leave never matched
another's. Not that they'd ever been that close to begin
with.

Carlos had an anchor. No, he *was* an anchor. It wasn't
the sort of thing to merely respect—it was something to
admire. She could feel the strength of it, the holding
power of that inner anchor so firmly set within him.

"Best part," he leaned back and paused while the
pizza was delivered and they each had burned their
mouths on the first searing bite.

"Is?" Sarah prompted him.

"Found a woman that I know I'm going to care about
just as much as all the rest of them. Even more, if that's
possible."

Sarah took another bite and decided that Carlos was
probably right about that, too.

Didn't mean she was going to make it easy for him.
But...yeah, he was right.

FLYING BEYOND THE BAR

US Coast Guard Rescue Swimmer Harvey Whitman lives to save lives. The unit's motto, "That Others May Live", defines his life's goal perfectly.

Helicopter Crew Chief Vivian Schroder, newly assigned to Astoria, Oregon, cares only for her career—and flying clear of her family.

When a storm-tossed nighttime rescue goes desperately wrong fifty miles offshore from the hazardous Columbia River Bar, they must rely on each other's instincts in ways they never imagined.

INTRODUCTION

Anyone who has seen the movie *The Guardian,* knows about Rescue Swimmers. It is a *hugely* popular film among the members of the Coast Guard because the filmmakers really went out of their way to get it right. (Reading the cast list down past the stars is looking at a roster of some of the very best the USCG has to offer as many real swimmers took on the roles.)

Aviation Survival Technician / Rescue Swimmer School has the same failure rate as the most elite Special Operations teams: SEALs, Delta Force, the 24th STS, and a few others. Under twenty percent of applicants make it through any of these courses. Even the 75th Army Rangers only have a sixty-five-percent cull rate. And the only ones allowed to apply to AST school are already some of the very best there are—yet still, four out of five fail to make the grade.

Their school starts with a twenty-four-week course. Graduates move on to EMT training, a six-month "apprenticeship", a week-long course in advanced helo operations like cliff rescue, and more. Overall, a mind-boggling set of skills to then be allowed to jump into the ocean in the middle of a storm, and try to save someone's life.

In choosing my victims...I mean characters, I wanted to show just how far a rescue swimmer will go. There is *no* thought of self, only of others.

And like so many at-home partners I've talked to (both of military and police officers), what does it take to love someone that dedicated? *Flying Beyond the Bar* was my attempt to capture that.

(And no, I have no idea where the graybeards in the bar came from. They just showed up and started singing.)

1

THE BEAT OF THE DOLPHIN'S ROTORS POUNDED INTO HIS body and Harvey Whitman did his best to tamp down the automatic adrenaline charge. The orange US Coast Guard HH-65C "Dolphin" search-and-rescue helicopter was hustling due west out of Astoria, Oregon and straight into the darkness of a Pacific Ocean nighttime gale. Blowing forty knots was so normal out here for a chill February night that the pilots hadn't even remarked on it as they'd loaded up. Something about the wild smell, the taste of the salt spray that a good storm kicked up into the air, always charged him up.

"Sea state is very rough," Vivian called out from her position as crew chief close behind the pilots but facing backwards into the cargo bay. A single strand of her dark curly hair had escaped the neatly formed bun to show between the lower edge of her flight helmet and the upper edge of the international orange survival suit they all wore. He'd always liked that curl. Even back before he knew Vivian Schroder's name, it had captured his attention. Not that the rest of her didn't, but there was something special about that renegade lock on the otherwise perfectly squared-away petty officer.

"Like that's news," Harvey didn't need to be able to see the nighttime ocean to know that. A Douglas Sea Scale State of 6, or "very rough" meant six-meter waves. Two-story high, wind-shredded surf rated as a typical dose of ugly for this stretch of the Pacific. "Just another day at the beach."

Vivian laughed over the intercom. Something she'd done every time he spoke his dad's ritual phrase.

"Just another day at the beach," Harvey recollected. *Sure, Dad. Except you were a Navy clerk for two years in San Diego and never spent a day on the water no matter how many tales you'd spun for all those years—before I figured out how to look up your service record.* Actually, confronting his father hadn't changed a thing: Dad's stories or his complete lack of interest in his son.

"Ten minutes," one of the pilots called back.

As the helo jounced through the storm, Harvey was glad to be doing the prescribed routine tasks. Thinking about his dad was never a good sign. He started prepping in case he had to go into the water. He double-checked the ankle, wrist, and neck seals on his wet suit. He'd already pulled the long beaver-tail of his jacket between his legs and attached it to the front of his jacket. Tapping the closures of his harness assured him that everything was in place. A habit-trained series of slaps located: radio, flashlight, knife, hammer for shattering glass with a hook for cutting straps, diver's knife, and magnesium flare. All in place.

He could see Vivian's eyes following the same pattern as she visually confirmed everything he touched.

"Anything new?" He knew that they would have told him if there was. That he would have heard the call coming in over the intercom. It didn't stop his need to know what he was getting into. Despite the drama in the movies, rescue swimmers didn't enter the water all that often and he wondered if tonight would be one of the exceptions.

"Nothing new," Vivian offered a lopsided smile at his need to know. Her smirk was almost as much of a tease as the stray curl of hair. "Fishing charter *Albatross*. It's a Bayliner 35."

He groaned to fill the pause she'd left for him to do just that. They all knew that Bayliners were designed to look good sitting at the dock. Smooth-water boats, they were never meant to go for deep-water halibut fifty miles offshore in February. Most of the Coast Guard's rescues were in the turbulent waters of the Columbia River Bar or hunting for people dragged out to sea by the coast's vicious rip tides. Where the river hit the Pacific was rated as the most dangerous shipping waters in the world and called for frequent assists within easy reach of the Guard's forty-seven-foot motor lifeboats. Not tonight.

"Six aboard." Which would load up the Dolphin to its capacity: the four crew aboard now plus the six rescued from the Bayliner. It was going to get tight in here fast. And that was assuming everything went well.

Of course they might not need rescuing at all. Most of the time it was a matter of telling them they were fine. If the situation was bad, their Dolphin's flight would pinpoint the endangered boaters so that a motor lifeboat or cutter could come out and give them a can of fuel or a tow. Only if it was dire would the USCG send a rescue swimmer into the water to help airlift them out.

A Bayliner 35 in two-story waves—they were probably just all too seasick to stand up.

2

"THEY WERE PROBABLY BLIND DRUNK." VIVIAN RECALLED Harvey's declaration about her parents at their first meal together two months ago.

"They probably came here first," she responded, because it was about the most unlikely circumstance on the planet. Her parents in an Astoria, Oregon bar was never going to happen. Especially not one like this.

Besides, it was Christmas Eve, always a big affair at the Adler mansion. Instead of surviving Mother's endless matchmaking, it was her third day in Oregon and Vivian had nowhere else to go. It was calm and unusually cold for the Oregon Coast—just below freezing, her breath had clouded on the night air as the whole team hustled out to Workers Tavern. It lay on a dirty back street under the Astoria-Megler Bridge that spanned the Columbia River between Oregon and Washington on the Oregon side.

The place was a total dive, and the owners were proud of that. Just in case there was any doubt, "Dive Bar" was

prominently displayed in the front window below the
glowing red-and-green "Breakfast All Day" sign and the
blue Pabst neon. Inside was deeply marine: dark wood
walls that might have been ripped off sunken ships, life
rings, oars, funky art, a mounted five-foot-long fish that
she didn't recognize but definitely declared "we grow
them big here", more craft beer logos than you could
count—though none so prominent as the big circular
Buoy Beer Co. sign.

Most of one wall was covered in small currency bills
from all over the world stapled to the wood. One of the
pilots had inspected them carefully and declared that a
third of them no longer even existed. The Australian
pound, the Taiwanese yen, Israeli lira—he listed off a
bunch of them. "And that's before you get into the
nineteen countries now using the euro."

"The place has been a port dive bar since 1926. Get a
lot of drunken sailors from a world of ports in that time."
Harvey had explained for her benefit.

Vivian wished she could get drunk. But both of their
crews were on call so they all had tea or coffee with their
prime rib—apparently a Workers Tavern specialty. The
air was thick with the smell of grilled burgers and fries
from the tiny corner kitchen tucked behind the massive
U-shaped bar. She, Harvey, and the six other Coasties of
their two helicopter crews had taken over one of the
battered tables close by the front windows.

The lead and backup crew didn't have to sit out at Air
Station Astoria, but they had to be available for
immediate deployment—which meant, "Don't leave town
and you'd better be stone cold sober." Quite how that had

turned into Christmas Eve dinner in a dive bar was something that still eluded her.

Sylvester and Hammond, her assigned pilots, had sworn this was the greatest place in all of Astoria. Having only just made it into town from the Aviation Training Center, she had nothing to judge by. The ATC, located in Mobile, Alabama, had also been far warmer. She'd wanted out of Alabama before another summer hit and had filed her request five days ago, knowing it could take months to fill. USCG thinking had figured that meant she should be posted to Oregon within the week in the dead of winter.

Astoria, Oregon? It was the sort of place that her parents had to look up on a map before properly showing their disdain, "Really, dear?" It had been their favorite phrase for dealing with their difficult daughter. Ambition was frowned upon for old Southern families. Especially the kind of ambition that had led her into the high school auto shop instead of the glee club or the cheerleading squad.

Then, to add insult to injury, instead of going to Clemson (where her sister had married a very eligible heir to a shipping empire) or the University of South Carolina (where her brother the lawyer had just proposed to a very popular US senator's daughter, practically guaranteeing his political career)—or even, God forbid, the University of Virginia (where she'd be at risk of meeting a Yankee stockbroker, but it couldn't be helped)—she'd gone straight to the Aviation Institution of Maintenance in that heathen hellhole of Las Vegas. It hadn't taken a genius to crack their code. Her parents had clearly looked up Southern schools with the highest "Meet Your Spouse Here" rankings.

Her parents had also tried to fire Captain Heath for "corrupting their daughter" with flying lessons in the family helicopter. She'd threatened to call the media rags with photos of both of her parents' flagrant affairs—not that she actually had photos, because...*ick!* But the threat had been sufficient to save Captain Heath's job and even up his salary.

The three years getting her Aviation Maintenance Technician Helicopter and two more working maintenance for Grand Canyon Helicopters had stood her in good stead when enlisting in the USCG. ("Maybe she'll at least marry an officer.") She'd decided to follow in Captain Heath's footsteps...but hadn't counted on that path leading to a dive bar on the Oregon Coast for Christmas Eve.

She'd been trying to explain her family to Harvey, for reasons that thoroughly eluded her. She typically did her best to pretend she was an orphan.

"They were probably blind drunk," was as good an explanation as any to explain her parents. She appreciated Harvey's levity, if not the probable accuracy of the statement. As if that would forgive any of the ways they'd tried to manipulate her.

Cocktails on the verandah at five. Mother would pour. Another one or two before dinner if there were guests, and there were always guests at the Adler's. Whether at the Mt. Pleasant house overlooking the first tee at the Snee Farm Country Club near Charleston, or at the country house out on Lake Marion two hours inland (half an hour by helo), they entertained lavishly—which included wine and after-dinner brandies. Father would pontificate. They were relatively new, banker money, so they put on far more airs than any genuine old-money plantation owner with ten times the holdings. Six generations back they had a Yankee, post-Civil War-profiteer ancestor that they kept far more hidden than their affairs. Father's family had "come into" large tracts of land surrounding Charleston, gambling on the city's recovery and expansion—a bet that had paid off very handsomely.

"They offered to buy a new building for my flight school, only if the president agreed to flunk me out first," was what she'd said that prompted his response about their state of inebriation.

Harvey's easy laugh fit right in at the dive's bar where a group of graybeards at the bar were trying to put together an unharmonious cacophony that would have definitely offended Wenceslas—whether or not he was a good king. They wore matching ball caps with pictures of beer steins on the front and the words "Christmas Cheers" in red-and-green glitter. They'd definitely had their share of Christmas beers.

She tried to read what lay behind Harvey's reaction. She didn't like revealing that she came from money—if her parents had bought the school a building, it would be far from their biggest investment that year. Revealing that wasn't her first choice. Or her hundredth.

Then why did you say it, girl? And to the overconfident Coastie she'd known less than forty-eight hours.

To shock the unflappable rescue swimmer? As if she

actually *was* more than she appeared because of her family's wealth? That was her parents' game, not hers. And if that was her goal, it hadn't worked at all. Instead Harvey looked around the bar and nodded to himself before cutting back into his prime rib—which she had had to admit was amazingly good.

"Pop would have liked this place," Harvey gave her a subject change. "I spent a lot of time as a kid in a place like this."

"You grew up in a dive bar?"

"Kinda. My pop sure grew old in one," his frown said she wasn't the only one with parents best left in the past. "But it literally *was* a dive bar down in Coronado, California. I made friends with the old, Vietnam-era Navy swimmer who owned the place. Joel trained me himself off the same beaches the Navy SEALs train from."

"And you aren't a SEAL because..." The graybeards hunched at the bar were onto something that might have been "Jumpin' Jack Flash" to the tune of "Jingle Bells." Or maybe it was "Yellow Submarine." Hard to tell.

He tipped his head as if cracking his neck. As if he was deciding whether or not to tell the truth.

She sipped her decaf coffee and waited to see where the coin was going to drop. Ten bucks would get her a hundred that he'd backpedal and cover the momentary lapse of honesty with another subject change.

Then he sighed and looked her straight in the eyes. "I decided, since I couldn't save Pop's life—even from his own, self-dug hole—that I'd rather save lives than take them."

3

"THREE MINUTES TO LAST KNOWN POS-*I*-TION," HAMMOND announced over the Dolphin's intercom from his left-hand command seat. There was a distinct hiccup in his voice when they slammed through an air pocket. Sylvester would be handling the bulk of the flying from the right seat.

The tightness in Harvey's neck wasn't going away. It could be three minutes to action or two hours before they had to return for a refuel if they couldn't find the lost Bayliner. Either way, they were in for a hard ride—the storm was still on the build and was slapping around the helo like a baby bird on its first flight.

"Permission to open doors?" Harvey called forward. It was never a good idea to surprise a pilot.

"Okay to open doors," Hammond acknowledged.

Harvey snapped a monkey line from his vest to a D-ring by the door and gave each end a good tug to make sure he didn't get thrown out the open cargo bay door by some nasty turbulence. Only after that did he unbuckle from the small jump seat at the rear of the cargo bay. Vivian remained belted into her seat, which could slide side-to-side so that she could work from close beside either door of the cargo bay.

What mattered now was eyes on the water. More than half the challenge of a rescue was finding the boat in the first place. The fact that there'd been no updates could mean that the Bayliner's passengers had simply forgotten to keep transmitting updates, that their radio's battery had shorted out, or that all that was left to be found was a couple of bodies kept afloat by their life preservers.

Vivian slid her seat all the way to the port side to watch out the massive window of the emergency exit door.

Harvey moved forward enough to unlatch the heavy starboard door. It edged out three inches, then slid backwards to slam into the end of its track. Before leaning out to look, he gave it a tug to make sure it had latched open and wasn't going to come sliding forward like a renegade guillotine when they hit the next air pocket.

"Gotta whole lot of nothing out this side." The pilots had the landing light shining forward, hoping to spot debris or even a smoothing of the wave surface from leaked diesel fuel. But looking off to the side, there were black clouds so thick that not even moonshine could make them glow. A hundred feet below them was the hungry maw of the Pacific waters that had eaten more than two thousand ships since Robert Gray first crossed the Bar in 1792, though Native traditions spoke of washed-up Asian and European ships all the way back to 1700.

"Oh, it's all bright and so purty out this side," Vivian announced breathlessly, actually getting him to turn and look. "Astoria looks like fairy lights at this time of night." Which was fifty miles behind them—five hundred feet would be a good visibility in this mess.

The woman had made him a sucker for a straight line. Just to rub it in, she wasn't even looking out the window as she said it, instead watching him turn and fall for her line. Yeah, she had him, hook, line, and sinker in more ways than one. He turned back to his own window to hide the smile that would have said just how much he was loving it.

Lives on the line somewhere below them, and still Vivian kept a cheerful and positive attitude. Harvey wasn't nearly as good at that as she was, yet another thing to admire about her. In the two months since she'd arrived in Astoria and they'd started flying together, it never varied. Nobody could be that consistently upbeat— yet it didn't feel like a facade.

When they'd lost that college student to stupidity on New Year's Eve. She'd gone quiet, but not downbeat.

The kid and his buddy had gone out on the beach at Seaside, Oregon to play around on an eighty-foot log at least four feet in diameter. Didn't they get that the ocean had put it there and could toss it around any time it wanted? There were plenty of signs posted to stay off the driftwood—but they'd ignored those. They hadn't even started drinking yet, so they hadn't had that as an excuse either.

The kid washed out to sea had been the lucky one, probably dead from hypothermia inside the first ten

minutes. His buddy had almost bled to death before they
could dig him out from where a sneaker wave had lifted
the twenty-five-ton log long enough for him to fall under
it before the water dropped it back down. He'd had to
have both of his legs amputated. They finally found first
kid's battered body washed up on boulders far out along
the South Jetty of the Columbia River, ten miles to the
north of Seaside.

No graveyard humor defense mechanism from
Vivian. Just a soft curse as Harvey had ascended from the
wave-beaten jetty on the winch with a body latched onto
his harness.

She'd helped him tuck the kid into a body bag
without flinching, then rested a hand on his arm. Just
rested it there until he could feel the human connection
through the thick neoprene swimmer's suit. Until he
could get past the first time he'd ever handled a dead
body in three years as a rescue swimmer. He'd lost
people. Saving two off a crab boat before it sank with the
other four hands already dead. But he'd never had to
recover a dead person before.

He hoped there was no repeat tonight because
finding that kid had been the New Year's present from
hell.

4

"THIS IS GETTING TO BE A HABIT," VIVIAN COULDN'T believe that she was back in Workers Tavern—ever. Being here for both Christmas and now New Years was just flat out unnatural.

Mother was threatening to fly out in the family jet to visit her baby girl. Maybe she'd bring Mother here. The graybeards would go crazy over the perfectly-maintained blonde-and-seriously-built Southern belle... Mother just might like that. Vivian blessed that she had taken the darker coloring and slender build of Father's side, allowing her to blend into the background a little better.

The graybeards' Christmas hats had been changed. Instead of two frothing beer mugs with "Christmas Cheers," their hats now had an empty mug and a full one on them and "New Years = New Beers" in silver glitter. They seemed uncertain about climbing the mountain of "Auld Lang Syne" and were now either doing injustice to ABBA's "Happy New Year" or slaughtering "New Year's

Day" by Taylor Swift to the tune of Judy Garland's "Over the Rainbow."

Tonight she and Harvey were off shift. Not even in the wings as the backup crew. They'd spent five hours in the air looking for the second boy before finding his remains out at the jetty. The Senior Chief had taken one look at Harvey and told her to take him out and get him drunk.

Having only been in Astoria for ten days, Vivian had taken him to the only bar she knew.

She'd had the French Dip with French fries. He'd had the French toast with bacon and sausage, but not risen to the bait of her teasing in French—even after he'd confirmed that he spoke a high school's worth.

An hour later they were still on their first beers. So much for getting him drunk.

"Tell me something, anything." It was the first time that he'd actually spoken first since they'd hauled that body aboard. Poor drowned boy. Senior in college which made her about three years and an entire lifetime older, except now his lifetime was done.

How did life get so short?

But that didn't seem like the right opener at the moment. She didn't know what to say, so she answered his question with a question, hoping it would help him get past whatever he was feeling.

"Tell me about that Navy swimmer. Joel, was it?" And apparently, she'd hit exactly the right topic.

It rapidly became clear that the young Harvey had taken all that love that his father hadn't cared about and heaped it on the SEAL sixty years his senior. It sounded so clear in his voice it might have been the ringing of a

New Year's bell, though he spoke no louder than enough to be heard across the table in a noisy bar. The aged regulars at the bar had descended to a vague form of karaoke, singing along with whatever Golden Oldies were being performed in the televised Times Square celebration where it was almost midnight already.

"Joel didn't know the meaning of half measures," Harvey actually finished his beer and ordered another. She was driving, so she kept nursing her first one. "He took me out to Catalina Island on the ferry one evening near sunset. All we had was a wetsuit, fins, and a snorkel. As soon as we stepped onto the dock, he pushed me over the side into the water. Figured we'd be doing a little recreational swim or something. I was fourteen and pretty convinced I knew everything I'd ever need to know by that point."

"Instead?"

"Instead he jumped in beside me, just bobbing up and down for a long moment, then he pointed out of Avalon Harbor toward the mainland."

She knew that a final, long-distance night swim was part of Rescue Swimmer training. There was a reason the Coast Guard rescue swimmers were considered to be the absolute elite. Them and the Air Force PJs—no one else was better. Their training course typically had an eighty percent failure rate.

But this didn't sound like he was telling a USCG tale. He was talking about something important. Honest men not just trying to get into her pants were outside her experience, but Harvey kept being that.

"I couldn't wrap my head around what he meant.

Despite the busy harbor and all of the crowded
waterfront restaurants and shops, all I can remember was
the silence down there on the water at the foot of that
long stone pier. It was so vast that it echoed. Joel just
looked at me and said, 'Well, you just gonna tread water
all night?' I thought about telling him to go to hell.
Instead, I took one last look at the comfortable ferry that
was still unloading, turned the other way, and started
swimming. Figured I'd show him just what was what.
Seventy if he was a day, he stayed right beside me the
whole way. Didn't speak again for thirty-two-point-three
kilometers. That's the shortest slice across the channel.
We actually swam closer to forty by where we finally
fetched up."

"How did you find your way?" He hadn't mentioned
having a compass.

"Stars," Harvey waved a fork up toward the bar's
ceiling stained black with years of smoke off the kitchen
grill. "I navigated back to the mainland using the stars.
The ships go every which way through that channel so
they gave no clues, though we had to avoid those as well.
From the height of a two-meter swell, the horizon lies less
than four kilometers away. That's as far as you can see
ahead even under ideal conditions—one-tenth of the
distance we covered. We finally fetched up on Balboa
Peninsula at Newport Beach seventeen hours later."

"*Seventeen?*" She tried to do an hour in the pool a
couple times a week. To swim for seventeen straight
hours in the ocean was... Vivian didn't know what it was
other than amazing.

"He didn't speak once that whole time until we

landed on the beach in front of those luxury homes and lay like a pair of dead fish. Our throats were raw with sea salt and dehydration. Our faces and the backs of our hands, the only exposed places, were sunburned lobster red. The hardest part was the last five meters, hauling myself out of the water and up onto that dry beach as a crowd of gawkers gathered around us. They actually called the cops on us like we were an invading force."

"What did he say?" What could Joel have possibly said that could tell a fourteen-year-old boy just how amazing he was, despite his father?

"He said, 'Now you know what *that* feels like'."

"He *what?*" Her shout was loud enough to get all the graybeards at the bar losing what little rhythm they had as they turned to look over at her. "He didn't tell you how incredible that was or anything?"

"Nope," now Harvey was starting to smile for the first time since they'd been called out on this morning's search for the college kid washed out to sea.

"I don't get it."

"Joel gave everything he had to teach me that limits are only there as long as we believe in them. Sure, what I did was a damned tough swim."

"Duh!"

"What Joel really showed me was that even at seventy he still didn't believe in limits."

It was only after she'd taken him home and they'd made love that night—because if Harvey the boy had been incredible, the man he'd become was amazing—that he returned to the story. As New Year's Eve midnight rolled across the Pacific Time Zone, with her curled up against Harvey and him toying with a single lock of her hair, he whispered so softly as if he was afraid the world would hear.

"He never swam again. Died less than six months later—fast, a stroke and gone. I always feel as if he passed the best of himself to me during that long night-and-day swim. After that he knew he was done."

She turned her face into his shoulder to breathe him in. He didn't smell of the ocean or even of wet neoprene that always seemed to permeate her skin for days after wearing a wetsuit.

"I keep thinking about that kid today. I'm wondering if someone had passed something on to him and now it was cut off."

"Joel gave you so much," Vivian almost felt envious. "All you can do is do your best to live up to that."

He considered, tugged lightly on the lock of her hair once more, then she could feel his nod.

As he turned to make love to her at the start of the new year as he had at the end of the old one, she knew what he smelled like. It was something she had so little experience with that it had taken her lying in his arms for hours to recognize it.

He smelled like hope.

"Ahoy! I've got a flare," Vivian's voice sang out loud and clear over the intercom.

Harvey's eyes actually hurt from the entire hour they'd been quartering back and forth across the violent waves searching for any sign. The silence had been as echoing as that long-ago day by the Catalina Island pier. The whine of the engines, the beat of the rotor, and the howl of the wind did little to penetrate the wall of six people's lives at stake.

Now a flare. Someone had survived. The helo must have finally flown close enough for the blacked-out boat to have spotted them.

In moments, they were hovering above the pitching craft. It was still afloat, but that was about all it had going for it. The waves—now at least the three stories tall of Sea State 7—were washing it end-to-end. All semblance of "pretty" had been ripped away: canvas, seat cushions, even the plastic windshields were now little more than twisted metal frames. The survivors were huddled miserably in the cockpit. At least they were wearing life vests, but how soon before hypothermia started taking them out—if it hadn't already—he couldn't tell from up here.

"What's the nearest cutter or lifeboat?"

"An hour out."

Harvey knew exactly what that meant. That boat didn't have an hour. They'd be lucky if it had fifteen minutes. "How much time do we have left?"

"Bingo fuel in twenty-seven minutes," Hammond called back. "Fighting the storm really is chewing it up."

"Let's get the basket moving! Diver off headset." Harvey didn't wait for the response before peeling off his headset and pulling on his swimmer's hood, googles, and snorkel. Once he had those secure, he began on his fins. He turned to shout at Vivian that they needed to deploy the lift basket *now,* but she already had it unfolded and was just waiting for him to get out of the doorway.

Perching on the edge, with his feet dangling out over the deep, he waited for her.

She slid her chair close behind him and locked it in place.

When her hand rested on his shoulder, the whole situation snapped into sharp focus. For six weeks since she'd first touched his arm after that failed New Year's rescue, the merest contact with her did that to him. Whether it was on a mission, walking down the street holding hands, or curled up in bed together didn't matter.

Right now, he could see the rise and slap of the waves. The way every fifth one slammed through with an extra ferocity. The sluggish wallow of the down-flooded hull. The debris field of canvas and lines dragging off the stern. All that crap served to make a sea anchor that kept the boat's bow pointed mostly into the waves—that's what had saved them. But it would be a death trap to a diver.

"Boat or water drop?" Vivian shouted. She didn't need to ask if he was going in. Any rescue was at the swimmer's discretion, but as long as there was a soul breathing down there, she knew he was going.

He was about to call for her to winch him down onto the boat when a wave slapped sideways across the boat and nearly tumbled it.

"Water."

"Definitely. We'll drop you upwind."

Harvey set his goggles and allowed himself to feel nothing but her hand on his shoulder. Listen to nothing except the quiet words they shared only in the deepest darkness of the night. Those moments together which oddly felt like when he'd been hanging with Joel. Vivian's arms were the place he was *supposed* to be.

The Dolphin had exceptional visibility for the pilots, but the final call was up to the crew chief, because only she could see directly below and even behind.

"Continue at four o'clock." They eased over and finally passed the boat. "Give me a nudge dead astern." She placed him exactly upwind.

He was just about to point out that he didn't want to be swept into the side of the boat by the very first wave that slapped him, but there was no need. Vivian continued her adjustments until she had the helo exactly where she wanted it.

She'd been doing the same to him—or perhaps they'd been doing it to each other. Six years in the Guard and he'd never flown with someone who he could so utterly trust. Not that the other guys had been bad. Nor was it that she was a woman who consumed his waking thoughts as thoroughly as she did his body, though she did. She was simply that exceptionally good.

"Were you top of your class?" Harvey had asked her one night as they lay awake with the dawn.

"Were you?" She shot it back short and sharp. Thankfully, her issues weren't his issues and he'd long since learned to answer those odd parental-reaction buttons of hers by remaining dead calm. It let her catch herself and cool down rather than heating up even more.

" 'A' School doesn't quite work like that," he'd answered her. "To graduate as an Aviation Survival Technician is half a year of learning to survive. If you survive, you're sent to a two-month EMT course and a six-month internship. Yeah, I could outswim the other guys, but that's about ten percent of being a Rescue Swimmer."

"Oh," she sounded deeply chagrined. Then she buried her face against his shoulder and he'd indulged himself in toying with her softly curling hair. She continued, "Getting to crew chief is a little different. Yes, I was top of my class and we were *insanely* competitive with each other." She said it like she was waiting for some judgement of why hadn't she somehow done better. She'd mentioned that the reverse putdown was also really popular in her family: "Oh, I guess the other people in your class aren't very good."

"Thought so," was all he said.

"Why?" she eventually whispered into his pectoral muscle.

"Because you're the best crew chief I've ever flown with."

"The best what?" She'd scooted up enough to take his earlobe in her teeth—hard.

"Flying with you is awesome," he held out.

"*And?*" She growled through clenched teeth.

"Oh yeah. I like your body, too."

"Harvey Whitman! You're—"

He'd never found out what he was, because he'd set about showing her exactly what he thought of her body and the wonderful things it could do to him.

"Swimmer ready?" She shouted over the roar of the rotors, bringing him back to the present.

He gave her a thumbs up.

"Deploying swimmer!" She held his shoulder hard for just a moment, as hard as when the releases shot through her shuddering body, then she slapped his shoulder and he pushed out of the helo.

Her timing was perfect, as always. The helo was hovering two stories above the wave tops, which was five stories above the troughs. A five-story fall into the sea would hurt like hell, ten stories would likely kill him. A two-story drop barely gave him time to grab his goggles with one hand so they weren't ripped off when he hit the water and wrap the other arm across his chest to keep his extra gear pinned in place.

The cold water was a hard slap anyway, but he was too pumped up to notice more than that. He surfaced with his raised thumb breaking the water first. By the time his head broke the surface, he slammed that raised arm into the water and speed-crawled down the wave face toward the boat. It took two minutes swimming flat out to reach it, despite body-surfing down the wave faces.

He hit the side of the boat, literally, but managed to grab the chrome bow rail one-handed. He yelled out against the wrenching pull as the boat lifted its nose high off the wave. If he let go, the bow could crash down on his head and the Coast Guard would need a new rescue swimmer.

Harvey hung on until the bow slammed down over the back of the wave. He let himself float up and executed a back flip over the rail and onto the deck as the boat buried its bow underwater.

On the next climb out of the water, he let the runoff sweep him along the deck until he reached the cockpit. There he slid sideways into the seating area and crashed into one of the people huddled there. Pretty clean entry.

"Hi there. My name is Harvey Whitman and I'll be your Rescue Swimmer today." The rote phrase marked the move to the next phase of the operation even as it consoled the survivors. "How are we doing, folks?"

He answered the question for himself. Three shaking so badly that they'd need a hospital soon if they were going to live. Two alert. One unconscious or close enough.

"We're going to be lifting you out by basket today."

"What about my boat?" Alert Number Two shouted

over the wind and the waves, identifying him as both the captain and a man without a clue. Portly was too kind a word to describe the man's massive girth.

"Let's worry about your people first, okay?" *And your boat is going to the bottom of the ocean any minute; you're an idiot if you don't already know that.*

6

VIVIAN NEVER TIRED OF WATCHING HARVEY WORK. THE world simply moved more smoothly around him. Even as he appeared to be calming someone, he casually raised an arm to signal for her to lower the basket, pointing to the downwind side of the boat.

She already had it hooked to the winch on the pylon just outside the cargo bay door. As the basket lowered, she kept a gloved hand on the wire. Part of it was so that she could feel any frays to the cable. It also let her dampen oscillations of the swinging basket and feel what the world's wind was doing, because it was hard to tell up here under the main rotor's downwash.

A wave slapped the basket, threatening to drive it into the group of survivors despite her lowering it on the downwind side of the boat.

Harvey grabbed it and wrestled it into place. All those miles he did in the pool every morning did far more than give him a magnificent body for her personal pleasure. It made him appear effortless in situations that mere mortals would be lucky to survive.

He'd taught her that so many times since they'd met. Not that he was exceptional—that was a given—but that *she* was. At first she hadn't believed him. But there was only so many times you could hear something and refuse to believe it.

That's what her parents, her family had done. For her entire life up until this last Christmas, she'd always been "less than." Harvey saw her as "more than." And he said it so often, that she'd come to believe it as well—almost.

Vivian could see that there was an argument down on the deck, which Harvey solved by bodily lifting someone into the basket, then spinning his arm over his head. For the moment he was touching the basket, she'd swear she could feel him right up the wire clenched in her hand.

As she reversed the winch to lift the basket and the first rescuee, she called to the pilots for a five-meter climb. The Dolphin had a four-axis autopilot that let the pilots set a hover and then spend their time paying attention to everything from remaining fuel to flying debris and rogue waves rather than fighting the controls. Bumping up the hover altitude during the basket lift added work for them, but it also got the survivor clear of the boat and the next wave faster.

The winch lifted the basket to be even with the door, but the survivor was a dead weight. She timed an air gust that robbed the helicopter of some lift and gave a yank just as the person went partly weightless. They tumbled to the cargo deck like an empty sack. All she could do at the moment was snap a safety line on the person and send the basket back down.

With every cycle of the basket down to the wallowing boat and back, each victim's condition became less acute —Harvey was sending up the worst first, exactly as he should. Frankly it was amazing any of them were alive with how little appropriate gear they wore. The Pacific Northwest winter called for wetsuits and Mustang float jackets, not a sweater and a slicker. The fourth one managed a muttered "Thanks" but was still shaking too hard to even crack her own heat pack. Vivian cracked one for her and tucked it in the front of her jacket. Warming up their extremities was too great a risk. She had to heat their cores first or risk making their maxed-out hearts fail.

On the fifth lift, Harvey nearly had to wrestle the remaining Survivor Number Six to the deck to let the basket rise. Because of the momentary delay, a wave caught the basket—heavily weighted with Survivor Number Five—and smacked it hard into Harvey's back. It sent him sprawling before she could get it aloft.

It took all the training the Coast Guard had ever given her to keep her cry of fear inside.

7

HARVEY SERIOUSLY CONSIDERED THROWING THE BOAT'S owner over the side and let there only be five survivors.

God damn, but his shoulder hurt. And his knee where he'd caught it as he crashed to the deck.

Whatever happened to the old adage of captain being last off? Letting the man go down with his ship sounded pretty good at the moment. Harvey had spent as much time arguing with the guy as watching the waves. Too much time.

It had taken Harvey a while to realize the guy was mostly drunk, just used to hiding it well. He'd certainly seen it on Dad enough times—the "functional" drunk. It should have made Captain Dan far more susceptible to hypothermia, but perhaps his bulk buffered him.

Foolishly, Harvey thought that the self-proclaimed captain made a good distraction from the decaying condition of the boat. The bow wasn't even lifting clear of the waves anymore.

However, being so distracted from his job that he'd let

a basket clobber him absolutely wouldn't do. He lay sprawled over what had once been the captain's pride and joy, the pilot's console with twice the number of controls and readouts than the boat really needed. Sound system controls, remotely operated searchlight (which the guy probably used for illegal night fishing), auto-pilot (that definitely should have been set to never let the guy leave the harbor), and more.

He shrugged a shoulder. Big damn mistake!

He dragged his focus back to the crisis; his head swam with a bout of nausea like he hadn't had since drown-proof training back in A School. He wasn't ready for the next wave that plastered him in the face and stole his breath away.

A chance grab at the steering wheel was all that kept him aboard as the biggest wave yet swept the boat. The other hand wasn't cooperating so well.

Something tried to push him aside. Then it thudded into his gut, but the blow was slowed by the water. Still, it drove out what little air he'd managed to catch. He was about to release his hold and hope he could follow the bubbles to the surface in the dark, when he resurfaced into the storm.

Beneath him, trapped against the deck between the console and the captain's chair, was the beefy boat's owner. That's what had hit him in the gut. But the prolonged dunking seemed to have taken most of the fight out of him.

The basket almost caught Harvey again on the next swing, but he managed to grab it, and heave the sputtering captain in. He was about to latch himself onto the basket and ride up with it from the doomed boat when his head cleared enough to ask the crucial body-count question.

"You're the last one, right? There were six of you. Right?"

"Six. Sure. Except for the dead one in the cabin."

Harvey's blood chilled. Something didn't sound right. If the others had survived out here in the elements, why would the one in the cabin be dead? He let his harness drop and waved the basket aloft.

"Harve—" Vivian's voice crackled over the radio. "We're bing...el in thre...utes."

"Roger, just have to check something."

"Repe—" was all he got back. Three minutes to bingo fuel, he didn't waste time repeating his words. Besides his bad arm was coming online now. The blow that had merely hurt, now screamed like a beast each time he tried to use his right hand.

The cabin door had been shut the entire time. The chances were that it was all that was keeping the boat afloat.

Watching the waves, he waited until they were sliding down the back of one. If he was right, once he opened the hatch, he'd have only ten to fifteen seconds before the next wave or two swept the boat under for good.

The boat punched through a wave rather than climbing over it. A chaotic cross wave actually rolled the boat, but he hung on until it righted itself. After it punched through another wave without going under, there was a momentary lull.

Out of the corner of his eye, he saw that Vivian had

lowered a lifting ring in place of the basket—far less likely to clobber him in the storm's growing chaos. Though he'd have to be sure to watch for the cable weight just above the hook.

He threw open the cabin door.

A truly nasty curse worthy of a severely pissed off crew chief crackled in over the radio, but it wasn't clear enough to understand so he ignored it. His radio must have taken a hit when the basket had struck him. His headlamp revealed a kitchenette on the left—with granite counters. Open cupboards revealed a pantry, well stocked with expensive alcohols. Couch to the right. Bed straight ahead in the forward point of the cabin. The water floated as high as the mattress—knee deep. No body floating in it.

He turned to exit.

Two doors that he'd rushed past on his way in.

Door Number One led to a closet.

Bank on Door Number Two.

A head—marine toilet. With someone slumped on the floor and hugging the commode, sitting in the water up to her chest.

Out of time, he slapped the woman hard on the cheek.

She coughed, sputtered, cursed. And reeked of whisky.

Alive.

Harvey grabbed her by the collar and fought her back to the deck.

She didn't wear a lifting harness, or even a life preserver.

Out of options, he snagged the lifting collar dangling from the helo's winch and shoved her arms and head through the opening. He slapped her again, brutally hard, even if it was left-handed.

"Huh? Whassup? I'm alive?" A trickle of blood ran from her lips. "Oh, wish I wasn't. My aching head."

"Stay awake and keep your arms down if you want to live. Do you understand?"

She nodded once, then again a little more convincingly.

He signaled Vivian to lift.

Nothing happened.

When his call on the radio went unanswered, he signaled more emphatically.

8

Vivian knew what came next.

Bingo fuel wasn't something that could be argued with. Helicopters were desperately unforgiving about running out of fuel. If they didn't want to punch a hole in the ocean themselves, they had to turn for shore right now. Any arguments about reserves in the tanks were always shut down—not even up for discussion.

"Is there a cutter closer than the shore?" she begged Hammond even as she continued lifting the seventh victim.

"No. Even if there was, we couldn't land on it in this weather."

"I have six aboard, Number Seven on the line. That's capacity."

"Good. Let's go."

"Swimmer is still in the water."

"He's what? Shit! Time?" Hammond wasn't asking about time until bingo fuel, he'd called that while Harvey was still in the cabin.

"Two full minutes to unload and cycle the winch back down. Have we burned enough fuel to take the extra person?"

"We're bingo now. Average weight?" Hammond asked, his voice betraying his own anxiety through his professional cool.

Vivian surveyed the rescuees piled up like cordwood on the helo's deck. "High. Very high." There wasn't a single person aboard who could clock in at under two hundred pounds and a couple were three-plus. And even as it ripped at her, she knew what she had to do next.

Hammond held the hover for a moment longer.

Vivian kicked out the raft package. "Raft away." The container wouldn't inflate until Harvey reached it. How many rafts had auto-inflated then blown away before the engineers had learned about that one?

Over the last survivor's head, she saw Harvey diving off the boat as it planed under the water. For some reason he was swimming one-armed toward the raft.

The boat never resurfaced.

9

HARVEY SAT IN THE WORKERS TAVERN WITH HIS ARM IN A
sling.

"No swimming for a month. How am I supposed to
stay in shape with one damned arm?"

"How is it that you're still alive to grouse about it?"
Hammond chided him but still sounded relieved.

Sylvester joined in the game, "Couldn't they have kept
you in the hospital longer so that we could eat in peace?"

Vivian just looked sad. He'd told her a dozen times
that he'd torn up his shoulder trying to heave the captain
into the basket, because she already felt too guilty about
having to leave him behind. She didn't need to know that
getting clobbered by the basket had started the problem,
then bodily lifting first the captain and then his wife—
who her husband had left for dead—had made it so
much worse.

Harvey definitely hadn't told Vivian about the bitter
thirty minutes he'd spent trying to get into the raft.
Once it had inflated, he could either hang onto it one-

handed or get aboard, but it had taken a slow trip through Hell before Charon the mythical boatman gave him a wave that he could ride into the half-flooded raft rather than dragging him across the river Styx into Hell proper.

He did consider telling her about *why* he'd managed to hang on though.

When the captain's wife had sobered enough in the hospital to understand that her husband had abandoned her for dead, all she'd said was, "That's my Dan all over."

After the challenge of getting on the raft, Harvey then had a three-hour wait for another helo to track down the raft's emergency transponder and come fetch him. At least they hadn't had to drop another rescue swimmer into the maelstrom, he'd been able to climb into the basket himself despite the storm continuing to build and his dislocated shoulder.

Riding out a full gale gave a man a lot of time to think.

"I—Shit!" He held a fork in his non-dominant hand and stared at his slab of prime rib. This one-handed lifestyle was gonna suck big time.

"Just jab it up and eat it caveman style," Hammond suggested, then made a show of cutting a neat piece and stuffing it happily into his mouth.

"Face down in it, dog style," was Sylvester's suggestion.

Vivian thumped the butt of her steak knife on the battered table and held it there with the tip pointing straight up. "Either of you want to try sitting on it? Don't think I can't make you."

Both of the guys were officers rather than enlisted and

outranked her by at least six inches to boot. But over the last weeks, they'd learned not to argue with Vivian.

Satisfied, she made quick work of cutting her own prime rib into bite size pieces then traded plates with him.

10

HARVEY STARED AT THE PLATE SHE'D CUT UP UNTIL VIVIAN wondered what she'd done wrong.

"We both had the *same* dinner."

He nodded but didn't look up.

"Not gonna feed you when you've got a perfectly good hand."

He shook his head, that wasn't it.

She glanced sideways, but Hammond and Sylvester were chatting up a couple of local women who'd sat at the next table over. Vivian might not have much experience at being a woman in addition to being female in a very male world, but even she could see that they were selling it hard: over-bright smiles, teasing giggles, shoulders up and back to display their figures to best advantage. Couldn't the guys see that? Maybe that's what guys *wanted*. Fine, let them fall down that hole and figure their own way back out. Her problem was the rescue swimmer across the table.

"What?" She whispered low enough to not interrupt the pilots' flirtations with doom.

"It's stupid."

"If that ever stopped you, you'd have left that Captain Dan to go down with his boat and gotten on the helo."

That earned her a brief glance and an almost smile.

"Explain yourself, swimmer boy."

He slowly forked up a piece of meat and began eating. "Death is a very strange thing."

"No shit."

"No," he looked at her as directly as he always did when he was talking about something important.

Vivian was worse than a deer in the headlights when he looked at her that way. She couldn't even look down to cut the next piece of her own roast.

"We don't talk about it. Swimmers I mean. It's the enemy. We drag people from its jaws. No matter the cost," he flapped his injured arm then winced as he made his point.

"*So others may live.* That's your motto. You embody that really, really well, Harvey." And it totally scared the shit out of her even if she wouldn't have him be any other way.

The entire flight back, she'd spent every second tending the seven rescues from the Bayliner. Core heat. Dozens of cuts and bruises from the battering they'd taken—blood welling up as they warmed. Not an instant to herself.

She'd finally got the captain to shut up about suing the US Coast Guard for not saving his boat—did it by ramming an empty flare gun up under his chin and threatening to blow his head off if he said another word. She'd heard Hammond's bark of laughter over the headset after Sylvester had turned around enough to see what she was doing and then explained it to his fellow pilot over the intercom.

It was the only laugh on the flight back.

Then off-loading everyone into the line of waiting ambulances. The debriefing, the mission reports, the… madness of not being able to go back after Harvey. Their crew had hit their airborne time limit because they'd done a beach patrol flight through the stormy afternoon. The standby crew had been headed aloft even as her bird had landed. But they'd had a backup hydraulic system failure thirty miles out and had to return before reaching Harvey so that they could change birds.

She'd forced herself to remain calm in the back of the command room.

When they'd finally found Harvey. And recovered him. *And* headed for shore. Only then had she allowed herself to weep. For the first time since childhood— Mother hadn't approved of emotions other than her own —Vivian had wept. Silently, by herself in the darkness of the empty Ready Room, she'd cried herself sick.

That had been this morning. Now they were at Workers again.

Hammond and Sylvester slid over to the next table, thinking it was their charm that was working on the two local girls, not the girls seeing two Coastie officers as their tickets out of whatever their lives were like.

"Swimmers never talk about Death," Harvey continued. Death was definitely a person to him. A personified enemy to be fought to the very limits. "We try never to think about it."

"But you did? Out there in that raft?"

"But I did." Again he looked down at his plate.

"What did you figure out?" Vivian was having trouble breathing. If Harvey gave up, she didn't know what she'd do. He'd made her believe that there was a "best" in people that was worth striving for. Sure, the world had plenty of Captain Dans. But a single Harvey could offset a thousand Dans. Ten thousand.

Harvey shoved around his cut-up meat bits for a moment, studying their patterns. Or maybe studying the depths of the ocean that he'd ridden over for those long hours alone.

"No one ever made a meal for me. Just for me."

"All I did was cut up your prime rib."

"My first memories were microwave dinners and bar food."

"Get a grip, Harvey." And the first thing she was going to do was cook him a real dinner. She'd learned from one of the best private chefs in Charleston, South Carolina. She hadn't learned more than the basics, but hanging with Chef Claude had made a good escape from her parents' pre-dinner social drinking. "You were talking about Death, not quite the same as a cut-up slab of beef."

Again he raised those dark eyes. "I knew that if I gave in for even a second, the ocean would swallow me up as if I'd never been."

Vivian couldn't suppress the cold chill that ran up her spine despite the warmth of the bar.

"I also knew that even if it didn't kill me, I could never face you if I gave in for even a moment."

"Me?" She felt suddenly breathless.

"Top of the class. Best lover a man could ever ask for. And," he stabbed up a piece of meat and held it out as proof, "kindness. A guy has to do a lot to deserve that. Women like you don't exactly grow on trees, Vivian." He nodded over to pilots' table where the flirting was fast moving into far more dangerous waters than they knew.

Vivian hadn't realized that Harvey was aware of what was going on around him. But he was a rescue swimmer. Except for that one brief lapse on the Bayliner, he had intensely trained situational awareness.

"No, we women, ah..." How was she supposed to answer a compliment like that?

We're like hothouse flowers. Except that was her mother —carefully cultivated and very well-tended, perfect as long as she was in her own little world.

We're few and far between? Was she? She'd never thought of herself as special. Not before Harvey anyway.

So...what?

"You're going to pick me from the tree."

"Thought I made that clear."

"Not very. What are you talking about?"

In answer he pointed behind her. She scanned the bar over her shoulder but didn't see anything unusual.

He pointed again, directly at the four aged regulars slouched together over their beers. They were wearing hats with two faces inside a sparkly red heart. They were working their way through Queen's "Crazy Little Thing

Called Love" that was almost in the right tune—as if maybe they'd even rehearsed it a couple of times.

That's when she spotted the date on the Budweiser calendar hanging on the wall. The picture was a stout and a pilsner in a red heart. It only took her a moment longer to realize today was the fourteenth, Valentine's Day.

But there was something more going on here.

Vivian felt an odd, floating feeling. There was something familiar about the graybeards' pink hats, though she couldn't imagine what it might be. In a daze, she rose from her seat and moved up to the bar, to where she was close enough to see their hats clearly.

Close enough to see the photos of the boy and girl inside the red heart. One was her. Not some glamor shot or official photo. It was her wearing her full kit, including her helmet and grinning at the camera—grinning at Harvey who had just told her that he loved her moments before a standard patrol flight two weeks ago. It had been one of the best moments of her life.

The other photo was Harvey plunging out of a helicopter: etched against the blue sky in his black fins and International Orange neoprene, going in to battle Death man-to-man. Someone on a sailboat had snapped the photo as Harvey had jumped in to airlift a heart attack victim to shore. The head-on shot was a powerful statement of "Help is on its way."

On the graybeards' hats, there was a small set of wings below the hearts. They spread wide from a circular center which contained crossed swimming fins—the Rescue Swimmer emblem.

The old guys were grinning wildly at her as their harmony swayed and clashed more violently than a storm-tossed sea.

A moment later Harvey's good arm slid around her waist from behind and pulled her tight back against his sling and chest.

"You're having them propose to me—for you?"

"Pretty romantic, huh?" Harvey laughed softly. "That's what I decided out there facing Death."

"What exactly?"

"So that *we* may live," he whispered in her ear as he reached up to tug on that one curl of hair he always toyed with.

He wouldn't be getting any argument from her.

CHRISTMAS OVER THE BAR

US Coast Guard Rescue Pilot Sly Beaumont lives to fly. Saving lives off the treacherous Columbia River Bar rates as a really cool bonus. As are the fine ladies who flock to the uniform.

Petty Officer Hailey Franklin may be new to the USCG cutter Steadfast, but she's a second-generation Coastie and knows all the guys' lines.

But when a storm-tossed Christmas rescue throws them together, neither one is ready for the lightning that strikes.

INTRODUCTION

Having (fictionally) driven a 47' Motor Lifeboat and flown a rescue swimmer into the storm, I thought it would be intriguing to look at what other craft the Coast Guard uses.

This "twelfth largest navy in the world" uses:

- The nation's ice breakers
- 18 different classes of ships, from 418' National Security Cutters to 65' Inland Buoy Tenders (yes, they take care of most of the buoys as well)
- The 295' three-masted tall ship *Eagle*
- 13 classes of patrol boats from 154' down to 16'
- 4 types of aircraft
- 2 types of helicopters
- Also drones and most of the offshore navigation radio stations (most of LORAN was decommissioned in 2010 in favor of GPS, but they still run the last five)

In other words:

- 240+ ocean and coastal patrol ships, tenders, tugs, and icebreakers

- 1,600+ smaller boats
- 200+ helicopters and fixed-wing aircraft

The USCG stationed at Astoria have only a small part of this inventory in operation, of course. But among that inventory are a pair of two-hundred-and-ten-foot medium endurance cutters. These ships can land a helicopter on their aft deck, though they rarely carry one full-time. And for fifty years they've proven just how tough they are. Perfect for protecting shipping over and around the Columbia River Bar.

In the previous story, I had created a couple from the helicopter back-seat team of crew chief and rescue swimmer. Like most of my stories, this would never be allowed under current military practice, families (even dating couples) cannot be in a common chain of command. However, having danced around that so often in the name of story and romance, it did seem time to find companions for my two pilots outside any chain of command issues.

In the first tale, Sylvester and Hammond had been flirting heavily with a couple of local girls. But I wanted to tell the story of the cutter as well. So, I brushed the girls aside (you'll see later that it didn't stick) and brought in two new members aboard the real-life cutter *Steadfast*. (My apologies to the crew and ship for any particulars I got wrong.)

Why specifically Sly and Hailey? Because they were just so fun together. I loved their interactions from their very first sentences in the car ride to meet their ship.

1

"THIS IS INSANE!" HAILEY FRANKLIN SHOUTED AT THE storm.

"When you're right, you're right." Vera replied from the passenger seat.

Hailey had met Vera Chu at the Portland, Oregon airport car rental counter. They'd gotten to know each other driving through the torrential December rain as they forged west to meet their new billet. Spending two hours together, squinting ahead into the darkness through the thick rivers that the windshield wipers on high couldn't clear, created a special kind of bond.

Their US Coast Guard cutter was berthed in Astoria, Oregon at the mouth of the Columbia River, which divided Oregon and Washington. And apparently it was crewed by fish who could live underwater.

"Perhaps there's a reason there are no scheduled flights to Astoria. Only a crazy pilot would fly on a night like this."

"You aren't the one driving," Hailey protested, not that

she'd given Vera the chance. When she was in any car, she drove. Ever since her brother had tried to drive under a tractor trailer full of lobster pots and sheared the top off the family car—with her in it—she'd insisted. She'd managed to pull him down in time, so it was just instant convertible rather than instant death...but still!

"I expect this is pretty in daylight." Vera had spent the drive announcing views that her phone map revealed but the pitch black storm hid.

All Hailey had seen for the last two hours was slashing rain on the twisty two-lane Highway 30. Half the time blinded by oncoming headlights and half with her own headlights reflecting off the walls of water that the Pacific storm was throwing at them.

By the time they reached town, her arms were sore from fighting the wind as it slapped their tiny Mitsubishi Mirage about like a hockey puck.

They'd determined three things during the drive.

Vera, the tall Chinese girl from Detroit, was the classy one. Not that Hailey cared. She was fine with being the short black chick from the farthest butthole of Maine. Why wouldn't she be?

They were both USCG born and bred, on both sides of the family, and were both carrying on the legacy by having just re-upped for their second five-year tour.

And third, the chances were good they'd be spending this next tour together. They'd both drawn slots on the USCG cutter *Steadfast*.

She figured that was good grounds for being best buds. Vera had reached the same conclusion even if she was, like, so slender and forever-tall. Though watching her fold into the Mirage economy rental had been pretty funny.

"You're aware that our ship is based from here," Vera asked as they arrived at the town limits sign.

"Shit! I thought we were just going for a scenic drive to a total nowhere town for the hell of it." Not even Astoria was as remote as where she'd been born. There wasn't a whole lot of America that existed east of Jonesport, Maine—the five hundred residents of Cutler and the Quoddy Head Lighthouse were about it. Maw and Paw had spent twenty years riding the buoy tenders along the coast and into the North Atlantic out of the USCG Jonesport Station.

"I'm simply curious regarding this place where we'll be based for a while."

"Won't see much of it. We'll be out on a cutter."

"This isn't the Navy."

Vera had a point. The cutter would mainly work the Washington and Oregon coasts, voyaging farther to sea only for search and rescue.

"Okay, let's see what we've gotten ourselves into." Vera had been navigator, not that there'd been any real questions. Out of the airport they'd had to make a grand total of one turn to pick up Highway 30.

There was a long silence. Long enough that the town lights were coming up.

"Um... As far as I can tell, the town is essentially one street wide and mostly in a two-mile stretch."

"Party town, whoo-hoo!"

"It means that the men are going to be small-minded provincials. Slim opportunities."

"Urban snob," Hailey teased her for her Detroit upbringing.

"Small-minded provincial," Vera teased her right back.

"Hey, just because I know how to haul a lobster pot and you don't, doesn't mean—"

"That's a pretty building."

"Columbia River Maritime Museum," Hailey read as they rolled by. "Could be fun."

"Oh!" they gasped in unison and Hailey immediately eased over to the shoulder of the road, stopping in a deep puddle.

Just past the museum was the dock...*their* dock. A pair of two hundred-and-ten-foot, Reliance-class Coast Guard cutters bobbed there. Also, an old-style emergency lightship—the kind with a major masthead light that could be driven out to sea in case a lighthouse broke and couldn't be serviced immediately. This one was a museum piece.

"At least we know we're in the right place," Hailey had always liked the Reliance boats. They were the first of the post-WWII cutters. Built in the 1960s, they had a sleek, determined look that said they'd been the workhorse of the Coast Guard for half a century and were still up to the task.

"We're not due for a couple hours."

"Food!" They declared in unison.

Yeah, spending the next five years hanging with Vera Chu could be a good thing.

2

"YOU LOST, SLY."

"Suck on it, Ham."

That was four times in a row that Lieutenant Sylvester Beaumont had lost the draw. He knew that his copilot Hammond Marcus was somehow rigging the game, but he couldn't tell how. This time it was their crew chief, Vivian who'd been holding up the chem lights, and still he'd drawn the red one.

Maybe...

He couldn't quite tell whether or not to trust her smile as she restowed the chem lights in their helicopter's emergency gear.

"Don't forget my horseradish this time, Lieutenant Beaumont," Harvey, their rescue swimmer called out.

"Blah. Blah. Blah." Sly had forgotten it once, like three months ago. Maybe it was Harvey's doing that he'd landed dinner-run duty four times running. The guy was quiet, but real sneaky. Yeah, perhaps it was *him* behind Sly's losing streak.

Harvey was sneaky in more than one way.

"Wedding just two weeks away. Got any nerves, Harv?"

"Not a one."

"Damn straight that better be your answer," Vivian paused in the middle of checking over her gear, long enough to pull Harvey down into a kiss. It quickly became clear that she was making it extra steamy just to mess with him.

"I'm outta here."

"About time," Ham grumbled.

Vivian's and Harvey's kiss broke up in laughter.

Totally messing with him.

He climbed into his pickup and headed into Astoria to get their dinner.

He didn't have a clue how Harvey had done it—and so damn fast. A total babe, Vivian had arrived on base last December 23rd. They'd been dating by New Year's Eve and engaged on Valentine's Day. Getting married on Christmas Day.

For himself, he had no real interest in slowing down yet, but he wouldn't mind that kind of lightning bolt striking him either.

And even though the Pacific Northwest wasn't much given to lightning, this Christmas Eve storm looked all set to deliver.

Wrong kind of lightning though.

There had been a pair of locals that he and Ham had been making good progress with—on that long-ago Valentine's Day. What with Harvey and Vivian getting engaged in their standard dive-bar hangout, it had set a definite romantic atmosphere for the evening—at least until Vivian had busted it up.

She'd sat down with the two hot townies and done the worst thing imaginable, told them the truth.

You girls want a good time, go for it. You want the long dream of escape from this town—because Astoria was the epitome of small town that most wanted to escape from —*Sly and Ham aren't your guys. The trick is, you've got to leave town yourself and go find what you're looking for. Take it from a woman who figured that out the hard way.*

And the two girls had. By the end of the month they'd both moved to Portland.

Vivian was a bad influence.

Vivian had made him think, though Sly hadn't mentioned a thing about it to Ham. Think a lot. (A *really* bad influence as that wasn't his normal mode.) And not exactly comfortable thoughts. What did he want long-term? Other than flying his USCG helo. What kind of woman was he actually looking for?

Damned if he knew.

3

"THAT'S A BRIGHT CHRISTMAS TREE," HAILEY BLINKED. THE thing was oncoming like major high beams.

Vera was doing one of her phone things. "Twenty-eight-foot artificial tree with four thousand LEDs in seven colors."

"Could use the thing as a lighthouse—for passing spaceships." Brake lights blanketed the road ahead of her. "What the hell? Who would traffic jam a one-road town on a stormy Saturday night?"

"That would be the Santa Swim."

"Santa Swim?"

"*Bring your Santa hat and float in our Aquatic Center pool for our annual screening of* Home Alone."

"You're kidding, right?" Then she thought about the blueberry costume parade for the Machias, Maine Wild Blueberry Festival. Maybe it wasn't so odd. Small towns did have their own quirks.

"There's also a Tuba Christmas concert tonight."

Hailey weaved her way through the traffic snarl and

made it out the other side. "If we didn't have to report aboard, that would almost be worth it."

"There!"

The car rental was on the main drag. And closed.

They hoisted their sea bags (that they should have dropped off at the ship) and dumped the key through the slot.

Just up the street, there were a number of cars parked close together, lit clearly by red and blue neon lights.

They shared a shrug and trotted that way through the downpour.

"Workers Tavern. Known for burgers and prime rib," Vera somehow ran, avoided puddles, and read her phone.

"Sounds spendy."

"It..." *more* phone thing even though the door was like twenty feet away "...isn't."

As soon as they were through the door, Hailey saw why. The bar looked as if it had needed a major renovation—for at least the last fifty years. Someone had done some recent work on it, but not enough to make it look any better than a total dive.

Perfect.

"They appear to all be different currencies," Vera was inspecting an entire wall covered in hundreds of low currency bills that had been stapled there. Hailey could hear her dripping onto the old wood floor.

Hailey was too busy taking in the marine ambience to check out the wall.

Buoy Beer signs—must be a local brew she'd have to try when she wasn't about to be on duty. Oars, ship's wheels, giant stuffed fish, a couple bowling trophies, so many signs it was impossible to make sense of them—though "Play Meat Bingo Every Sunday" definitely stood out. Only one television, and it was off. Definitely her kind of place.

Battered tables to the front and a big U-shaped bar to the back. Good crowd. Not packed, just cozy and friendly. Group of old graybeards at the far end of the bar harmonizing Christmas carols with no apparent melody and few discernable words.

By the amazing grilled-meat smell coming from the corner kitchen, they'd definitely hit pay dirt.

They dumped their gear and slicks in a corner that didn't look too grotty, then took a pair of stools at the bar.

"Beer?" The barman had a generous beard, shaved head, heavy earrings, and an impressive set of arm tattoos. He also stood about six-five and had a good smile.

"I wish. A Coke and a steak. Still mooing."

"Coastie?"

"Why do you ask?"

"No one except a Coastie comes in here asking for a Coke with their steak."

"Two of us." She nodded to Vera who ordered a burger and a pot of tea.

The barman just laughed and headed to the kitchen at the back of the bar.

"Tea, really?"

Vera just shrugged pleasantly.

4

SLY WAS SO PSYCHED.

Ham was totally missing out and he'd get to rub it in for the whole upcoming flight.

In a town not known for having a lot of variety—especially because their crew kept coming to this same place to eat and drink—there were two new women at the bar. With their backs to him, he took his time moseying up to the bar.

He spotted the luggage covered in slicks. Mega-bonus: they'd just hit town. Too bad he was flying tonight. Maybe they'd be around for a while.

One was tall and had straight, jet-black hair down to her shoulders.

The other, much shorter, clearly had curves, and super-curly hair cut short.

"Hey, Teddy," he sidled up to the bar. He handed over the order because he forgot to call it in. "And Harvey is whining about the horseradish again. Could you give me a container of mayonnaise instead or something."

"And mess with my man, Harvey? Dream on," Teddy grinned and headed back to the cook.

Then Sly turned. From the front neither bar babe disappointed.

As advertised from behind, the tall one was sleek. One of those Asian types—Chinese, Japanese, whatever. He could never tell.

The short one did indeed have curves, great ones. Lushly dark skin, and a sideways grin that said she totally knew that he was checking them out.

"His name's Teddy?"

"No, but he's built like a giant Teddy bear, so it works on him."

"Less than you'd think." The bartender planted a glass of water on the bar, hard enough to slop some onto Sly's arm—not that it really mattered with how wet it was out there.

Teddy's wink at the women proved he'd done it on purpose. Sly really didn't need the trouble and waited until he'd moved off to pull some pints at the other side of the bar.

"So, you here for the surfing?"

The Asian chick looked at him in wide-eyed mystification.

The curvy black chick almost snorted her Coke with a bright laugh, so he riffed on it.

"It's big here on the Coast. They even have an app that announces when and where the surf's up."

"It's December, dude." Her voice was low and throaty. Nice.

"Wetsuits. Year round. Honest," he raised a three-fingered Boy Scout salute.

"What? You made Tenderfoot? Can't believe they let you in at all."

"I got to Star."

"Oooo, Vera, we're in the presence of greatness. Too bad he flunked out before he made Eagle Scout."

Well, that gave him one of their names, but the wrong one.

"Actually, I had to choose whether I went Eagle or started lessons in—"

"Remedial 'Being a Human Being'?" She was quick.

"Yeah, that." He gave her a nod, conceding the round. —*flying lessons*. At least that's where he would normally work being a USCG helo pilot into the conversation. But he liked her quick response too much to ruin it.

It lit up that killer smile again. "So, you're, like, Mr. Surfing Man?" She held out her arms as if she was balancing and riding the waves.

"In this weather? Shit no. I'm not that crazy."

And her laugh gave him that round.

Teddy delivered the babes' dinners, so closely followed by a bag of his four orders that it was clear Vivian had called it in. Damn, just when he wasn't in a hurry.

Teddy tossed Sly one of those small plastic containers. "Don't be losing that, or you really *will* piss off Harvey and I wash my hands of whatever he does to your sorry ass. Mayo's in the order, that's his horseradish."

"Dude!" He held up a hand for a high-five, which Teddy

ignored just long enough to make the bar chick laugh again, before delivering. Damn but she had a great laugh. Sly then tucked the horseradish container in his slicker's pocket.

"You going to be in town a while?"

"Yes, we are," Vera replied calmly before cutting off a bite of her hamburger—with a knife and fork.

"A fair bit," the other one mumbled around a mouthful of prime rib.

And for some reason he didn't understand, he decided to just play it cool. As if Vivian was watching over his shoulder and telling him not to mess this one up.

"Well, gotta go feed the wolf pack before they get too ravenous," he hefted the bag to make his point.

She waved a knife at him in goodbye as if he was totally unimportant.

"You got a name?" Sometimes you just had to ask.

"Yep. You?"

"Uh-huh."

"Good thing to have," then she made a show of sticking another bite of prime rib in her mouth before turning to her friend.

Only after he was out the door did Sly realize that he hadn't played his best card. "Coast Guard helicopter pilot" never failed to wow the ladies. Though maybe *not* with this one. She had a whole lot of different going on.

5

"WELCOME TO THE AVIATION DETACHMENT ABOARD THE Cutter *Steadfast*," the captain had greeted them.

Then he scowled down at them dripping on his pristine bridge deck. The storm had abated enough that they were merely drenched rather than needing gills after the hundred yard crossing from taxi to ship. *Drowned rats asking permission to come aboard, sir.*

"I assume you know your duties when a helo is aboard. Chief Mackey will make sure you know what to do, otherwise."

That and a salute was the entire scope of their welcoming ceremony. The captain was definitely old school. *Yeah, just two new overeager petty officers to worry about.* With a total crew of only seventy-seven Hailey thought he would have at least asked their names.

The captain probably appreciated them arriving together as it saved him repeating his lengthy greeting.

After him, Chief Petty Officer Mackey, a taciturn San Diegan probably built rather than born on the Navy base there, had showed them where they'd be bunked together. As they dumped their bags, the chief had given the entire ship's tour—which had consisted of him asking one question, "Been aboard a Reliance-class boat before?"

When they'd both nodded, the Chief was nearly as brief as the Captain. "Good. You're the new AVDET team. Prior team rotated out this morning, so no handoff, but you know your duties. Stow your gear, get flight squared away, and then get some sleep." He'd know they'd both just crossed the country from Little Creek, Virginia, and Pascagoula, Mississippi. Which meant, on military transports that never connected the way passenger flights did, neither had slept in two days. Still, first priority was readiness. Sleep was a distant twenty-fifth on any action list.

Coast Guard cutters weren't big on sitting still and the two-hundred-and-ten-foot *Steadfast* was no exception. It had started moving out of port an hour after they'd boarded. Command must have said to start the patrol on today's date and the captain had interpreted that as straight-up midnight rather than daybreak. Hard-charger or total jerkwad had yet to be seen.

By the time they hit the flight deck, *Steadfast* wasn't so steady. She was nosing out of the Columbia River and into the Pacific. The last lights of the North and South Jetty were blinking away dead to starboard and port. Mid-channel markers slipped by in red and green. A peek over the side rail revealed nothing but churning waves.

The seas, which had been slapping the cutter side-to-side was now intent on porpoising her up-and-down as well. It took major waves to do that to a Reliance-class ship.

Full slicks, life jacket, and double safety harness, they'd split up at the rear hatch to survey the status of the flight deck.

Hailey uncoiled and recoiled a couple of tie-down lines just to make sure that the lay of the line was clean and wouldn't snarl if she needed them fast. She liked when she spotted Vera doing the same on the other side of the deck.

Together, they inspected the refueling and rearming status—everything at full inventory. Toolkit was good and spare parts were few. Made sense because a boat like the Reliance rarely carried a helo full time. She could cruise for eight thousand miles between resupplies, but probably rarely ran more than a hundred miles off the coast.

In silence, they did an FOD walk—more an FOD stagger, weaving like drunks back and forth across the pitching deck. No foreign object debris.

Because the HH-65 Dolphin's engines sat high atop the fuselage, it was unlikely that they would suck up any damaging debris. But the heavy blast of a helo's rotors could turn the smallest bit of junk, such as a dropped bolt, into a painful missile for the deck crew. Or even worse, roll underfoot at the wrong moment.

But the deck was clean, and they finally met at the stern rail. The thirty-by-sixty-foot deck was their main domain.

They gripped the stern rail as the bow nosed down into yet another deep trough lifting them several stories into the air. The lights of the four-mile-long Astoria-Megler Bridge, arcing high out of Astoria before touching down in mid-river to continue to Washington, was just visible through the storm.

"This is insane!" Vera repeated her call from the drive out. Now it was almost inaudible over the hard pounding of the rain, driven bullet-loud against the back of their slicks.

"When you're right, you're right," Hailey gave the same reply and they both laughed.

But neither of them moved.

For Hailey it was a blend of exhaustion and exhilaration. Maw and Paw had done their twenty years for the Coast Guard, retiring when she left grade school. They'd moved eighty miles south to teach at the prestigious Maine Maritime Academy in the relative metropolis of Castine—population of thirteen hundred plus a thousand students.

And here she was doing *her* dance.

As she watched the lights of their new homeport fading astern, she couldn't help grinning. Cute guy within an hour of arrival. Not too shabby. Funny too. Major, *major* points for not going for her phone number, or push for her name.

Like he thought they were fated to run into each other again.

The fates of her past had proved pretty damn fickle. The only thing that had held true was the Coast Guard. The men sure hadn't. She'd been hit on by married officers, too crass to even pull off their ring first. At least their new captain hadn't done that.

"Why do so many men assume I'm easy?"

"Looking the way you do, you're surprised?" Vera answered even though Hailey hadn't meant to speak her question aloud.

"What? Why?"

"Hailey. You're beautiful. I'm like this total stick figure of a woman."

"A totally elegant one."

Vera shrugged uncertainly enough for it to show through her gear. "I'm not the one he hit on."

"Mr. Surfing-dude Boy Scout? He's a total hound dog, couldn't you tell? That's what I always draw. Guy who falls for *you* will have a weak spot for pure class. I couldn't wear class even if it came in a dress my size. And trust me, it doesn't."

"So, what happens if you run into him again?"

"Not gonna happen. We're headed out on patrol."

Vera's shrug this time indicated something else, but Hailey wasn't sure what.

6

"THURSDAY. THIS HAS GOTTA BE A THURSDAY."

"It's Tuesday. You and I go off rotation on Thursday."

"Oh, that's why I always thought Thursdays sucked. You sure this isn't a Thursday?" Sly would *always* rather be flying—except maybe tonight. The hangar's inside worklights barely made it out the door. Beyond the windshield of his US Coast Guard HH-65 Dolphin helicopter the sideways rain slashed even harder off the Pacific than when he'd done their dinner run. As the engines continued spinning up, he decided that the night looked very, very Thursdayish no matter what Ham said.

Air Station Astoria was defended from the direct onslaught of the Pacific storms which slammed the Oregon Coast by sitting three miles inland. The problem was that the high point in that three miles was all of eight feet above sea level. The airport lifted a full yard higher into the wind at eleven feet. The stunted coastal pines had been kept well back from the west side of the airport, so offered little defense.

"The storms know, they just know." He continued checking the items on the pre-takeoff checklist as Ham called them out from the copilot's seat.

"Know what? N1 at release?"

"Starter released. They know just how to swing into the mouth of the Columbia River so they can hit us with a straight shot."

"You're now manifesting this poor, little, innocent storm with evil intelligence to make up for your weird Gloucester Nor'easter superstitions? You're a real sad dude, Sly. Engine and transmission oil?"

"Check and rising. Just like this damn storm's temper. Innocent, my butt. Why do people have to go out to sea and get in trouble on nights like this? Why can't they just all stay home?" Sly could hear his past sneaking into his own voice. He still remembered the nine days huddled with Mom until they'd found Dad's fishing boat—or what was left of it—washed up on the remote Sober Island along Nova Scotia. "Unlikely-sober" Island as Mom had called it ever since.

Tonight, the inevitable call came in: crab boat in the shit—and sinking.

"Because if they did, we'd be out of a job. Nav lights, caution breaker, fuel boost?"

"On, in, and in," Sly tapped each switch and circuit breaker to confirm it and kept his tone light. "You're right. That would be even worse. Then who would pay us to fly?"

"Well, no one would pay *you*. But I'm such a handsome and charming brother, they'd keep me on just to make the Coast Guard look good."

"The only way you'd ever look good, Ham, is if they slipped a different corpse in your casket after you died." There'd been a debate ever since they'd hit the same air station on the same day two years back: which of them drew in the women, and which repelled them. Their far superior success as a team made it difficult to keep any meaningful score—not that it stopped them from trying.

He'd long since learned that pointing out his last name, Beaumont, meant "pretty mountain" was a bad idea. *Talk about mountains out of molehills,* Ham had instantly replied. *You know, you do kinda look like a mole.* Yeah, so not worth the effort. And he couldn't do much with Ham's last name of Markson. And he was a damned handsome black dude. He'd have to make sure *not* to introduce him to the sassy girl in the bar if he did manage to run into her again.

They were all the way down to anti-ice system check, which they'd be bound to need in the December storm, before Ham tried again.

"ELT check? We gotta watch the bar."

Sly glanced over. How could Ham know about the total babe? He hadn't been there.

Oh, the Bar (Captial B). The Columbia River Bar.

"Check." As always, he sent up a brief prayer to Mama's God asking that they wouldn't need the Emergency Location Transmitter tonight. It would only be needed if they crashed.

The mouth of the Columbia River Bar was also known as the Graveyard of the Pacific. The worst and most dangerous stretch of shipping water anywhere in the world. Even the Straits of Magellan at the southern tip of Chile were more traversable. They also had a lot less traffic, instead of servicing three of the top fifteen US agricultural ports like the Columbia. Not to mention enough recreational boaters to make a man choke on his soda.

"Yeah, the Bar." On a night like this—with the Columbia dumping two million gallons of water per second into the ocean, and the storm surge, not to mention the high tide ignoring all that to try for Portland way upriver—there was bound to be some major ugliness. Except the call had come in from much farther out to sea.

"Instruments all normal?"

There was a long silence as they both double-checked for any bad instrument readings—from compass to engine temperature to altimeter (which revealed a depressingly low barometric reading for eleven feet above sea level). There weren't any problems because the Dolphin was an awesome search-and-rescue helo.

"All normal," Sly reported per the checklist then called back over the intercom. "You two still with us?"

Harvey the rescue swimmer grunted an affirmative. Guy hadn't even tasted the mayo. He'd taken one look at it, then held out his hand until Sly placed the horseradish container in his palm. He'd now be belted in at the very rear of the cargo cabin.

Vivian's seat placed her facing backward directly behind his own position. She reported by the numbers because she was that kind of squared-away gal.

"Wedding is Christmas Day. Can we trust the two of you to keep your hands off each other back there?"

"Can we trust you two to keep *your* hands off each other?" Vivian shot back.

"Only because it takes two hands to fly," Harvey offered one of his rare comments.

"It's Sly," Ham joined in. "He can't stand that I'm the pretty one."

"Just get us out there," Vivian gave a long-suffering sigh.

"Your wish is my command, oh Queen of the Skies."

He eased up on the collective, rocked the cyclic forward, and climbed up into the darkening sky.

7

"HOW LONG WERE WE ASLEEP?" VERA GROANED.

Hailey checked her watch and sighed, but put on her most cheerful tone. "Almost two hours. What's your problem, Vera?"

"I'm not some android like you is the problem. I need at least two-and-a-half hours to recharge my batteries."

They dressed fast and reported to the bridge as ordered.

Despite the late hour, the captain was on deck. As well as the XO, two helmsmen, a navigator, and a radio operator. Chief Mackey arrived moments later.

The captain waved them over to the chart table.

"Franklin. Chu. Glad to see you're not sickers."

So, the fact that they didn't puke in bad weather had earned them "named" status in the captain's book. Hailey was okay with that. Because if the Reliance had been lively before, now she was positively active. Quartering waves, with the engines now running at full turns based on the vibration through Hailey's boot soles, gave the

Steadfast a funky, hip-hop beat motion—one that Hailey's Maine heritage had never been able to follow on the dance floor. However, on a boat? No prob.

"We're in pursuit of the *Savannah Jack*. Forty-six-foot aluminum crabbing boat that's lost its engines and is in imminent peril of sinking. Crew of five. She's over two hundred miles out."

Mackey cursed, "How the hell did they end up that far offshore?"

"Unclear. Drunk, asleep, driving for Alaska in too small a boat? Who knows. We will *not* arrive in time."

That earned him silence.

"There's an HH-65 Dolphin enroute. Our mandate is to get as close as we can to serve as a landing platform."

Hailey didn't have to do the math. Vera's look said she'd reached the same conclusion.

A four-hundred-mile round trip was close to the helicopter's total range. If they had to linger onsite for a rescue, they wouldn't get back to land. Every mile closer the cutter could get to the crabber was that much longer the helo could remain on-station at the sinking.

"We've checked over everything on the flight deck, sir. We're as ready as we can be for a landing in this kind of weather."

"You will not be losing me a helo on your first day. Are we clear on that?"

"Yes, sir," she and Vera snapped it out in unison.

"Then we understand each other. I let you sleep as long as I could. The helo is already at the *Savannah Jack*. They were able to locate her immediately thanks to the crabber having an ELT. We'll be out past fifty miles by the time the helo will be coming back. They're winching aboard the last crewman and the helo's swimmer right now."

"Must be hell out there," Mackey grumbled.

There was a brief silence as they all sent prayers or whatever was needed out to the rescue swimmer down in that turbulent mess.

"They'll be here in under an hour. Recruit whoever you need, get them safely onto my deck."

"Yes sir."

"I'll send you a pair of MEs," Mackey said before waving them aft. Maritime Law Enforcement Specialist meant a sailor who was good at thinking fast on their feet in chaotic environments.

Hailey could get to like Mackey.

8

"WELL, THAT WAS FUN," HAM ANNOUNCED.

Even with the two of them and the four-axis autopilot the rescue had been a major battle. Even clear of the land effects, the waves and wind had been in a contrary mood.

Harvey and Vivian had done their usual amazing task. Harvey had dived into the fray, eventually recovering two bodies and three survivors. While they worked frantically to save the latter from hypothermia, it was now up to Sly to get them to the cutter *Steadfast*. Quickly.

But getting there fast wasn't the problem. They had a ferocious tailwind, which was a good thing. If it had been a headwind, as it had on the way out, they would be in even worse trouble than they were. Having his only available refuge being a hard-pitching cutter just five times longer than his helo was not a comfortable thought tonight.

"Cutter *Steadfast*. This is Dolphin 58 inbound," Ham called ahead on the radio.

"Roger, 58. Winds forty, gusting sixty. Waves at thirty, chaotic." *That* was the problem. Landing on the pitching helo deck.

"Roger that. We'll need immediate medical for the three survivors. Crew plus five aboard." A nice way to say they had two in body bags.

"Sounds like this is going to be even *more* fun." Sly couldn't see a thing out in the utterly foul night and was completely dependent on instruments. Storm dark. Moonless storm dark. And they were still fifty miles to the ship.

"Sure thing. And I'm not looking for a swim, so try actually landing on the deck this time."

Back during training, Sly had misread the markers on the airport runway that were supposed to be the outline of a ship's deck. So, he'd landed *beside* the theoretical ship rather than *on* it. Five years, and Ham hadn't let him off the hook on that yet. "It was my first landing, for crying out loud."

"Whine. Whine. Whine," Ham teased as he entered *Steadfast's* latest GPS coordinates into the onboard systems. "Fifteen minutes," he called back to Vivian and Harvey.

"Okay," Vivian's calm response was a good sign for the three survivors. Not that she was ever *not* calm. But if things were still going badly, she'd be too focused to even hear them.

"Man, that's gotta be a rough ride. *Steadfast* is coming toward us at full steam."

Sly eyed the fuel gauges and hoped that she really

was. He had reserve fuel, but he'd have to land dead clean if he didn't want to get caught depending on it.

He hoped he could make it back to shore tonight. Maybe swing by the Workers and see if the nameless woman was still there, crooked smile and all. Wicked hot, but...he hadn't really looked at her body once he'd heard her laugh. Weird thing to stick in his head. He hadn't even lorded their meeting over Ham, which was not like him at all.

Whoever she is someday, Sylvester, Mom was the only one to always use his full name, *make sure she's someone who does* not *go to sea.* She'd never really recovered from Dad going down. Of course, Sly couldn't imagine anyone being prouder or bragging more on her son, than when he'd qualified as a helo pilot for the Coast Guard.

Or more afraid.

9

WITH THE PERIMETER FENCE AROUND THE FLIGHT DECK folded down and Astoria nowhere in sight, Hailey felt a hundred times more exposed.

Her first tour had been out of Virginia Beach, Virginia. She'd ridden out some rough storms—tail ends of hurricanes and such. But Mackey had said that tonight was nothing out of the ordinary. *Just five thousand miles of open Pacific come to piss on us.*

Clearly, this posting was going to have a whole lot of new experiences for her.

Experiences like the guy in the bar?

Vera had only brought him up about six more times —in that quiet way of hers. As if Hailey wasn't thinking of him enough on her own.

She'd lived in enough small towns to see how completely he stood out in the crowd. Hell, he'd stand out in any crowd.

Hailey again checked the deck. Between them, she and Vera had decided to take turns as the lead Landing

Director. She'd immediately claimed first right by order of the alphabet.

"Hailey wins out over Vera."

"What about Chu over Franklin?"

"H plus F equals eighth plus sixth letter of the alphabet. V for Vera plus anything is like a kajillion. My win."

Now she stood at the forward end of the open flight deck and wished she'd gone second. Tonight's landing on the pitching deck was going to be a nightmare.

Vera stood off to the side with a pair of unlit batons just as backup. The two MEs were squatting off to either side. They knew the drill, but she and Vera had gone over it with them again anyway. They'd spent half an hour talking through escape routes if something went wrong, firefighting in case whatever it was went *badly* wrong, and every other scenario she could come up with. Besides, it beat the hell out of waiting and wishing she was still asleep.

"This is Dolphin 58. Have you in sight, *Steadfast,*" sounded over the radio headset built into her safety helmet.

"Say again," Hailey couldn't believe it. She knew that voice, but couldn't place from where. She hadn't heard of any of the guys from her last station at Virginia Beach transferring out West. No, it was more recent than that.

Swiveling around, she spotted the helo coming to hover off the port side.

"Belay that. Roger in sight."

Not quite hover, as the ship would be driving ahead at fifteen knots and the wind blowing the other way at forty-plus. He was actually flying at sixty knots and looked as if he'd been bolted into place against the vast blackness. The pilot was so steady that it was the first time she was really aware of how badly the deck was heaving about.

Her body knew what to do with the pitching deck, but her eyes tracking the helo back and forth were less sure.

"Captain, are we dead into the wind?"

For the moment, she was the master of the ship.

"If this wind *has* a dead into, we're there," he called back. She could feel him up on the bridge, maybe out on a wing in the storm, watching his newest crews' every move.

She glanced behind her to make sure that she was exactly in front of the foot-wide yellow stripe painted up the aftmost bulkhead. It marked the center of the ship and the center of the Flight Deck for the pilot.

A hard gust and her gut told her that the boat had just made a fierce twist from slamming a wave.

Just gotta surf it smooth.

And then she knew exactly where she'd heard the pilot's voice before.

10

THE LAUGH OVER SLY'S HEADSET WAS AS BRIEF AS IT WAS unique.

"You've got a sick idea of fun, Ham."

But it wasn't Ham's laugh.

Sly had never put down on a deck when a ship was as breezed up as the *Steadfast* was doing. This was gonna be savage.

He briefly wondered if the nameless woman in the bar danced. He sure hoped so. She'd be something to watch.

And she'd have a laugh like...

"Ha!"

"What?"

"Nothing, Ham. Tell you the joke later.

Green baton pointed to the left, the deck crewman— the nameless bar girl, new to town, USCG new to the *Steadfast* (damn but that *was* really funny)—began waving him inboard with the red.

He shuffled over until the yellow stripe was dead

ahead. The problem—that the H at the center of the helipad was rockin' and rollin'—was the baton wielder's problem.

For now, he set aside everything except what she was signaling for him to do. It was one of the hardest things for any pilot. He could see the boat pitching, but he'd never be able to anticipate it well enough to land.

This required absolute trust in the person on deck guiding him in.

Sly shoved aside how much he didn't know about the woman, he locked his attention on staying centered on that yellow stripe of the ship's mid-line, and focused on her two batons.

Down...hold!

Hold.

Hold.

Down! Hold!

He found her rhythm easy to follow.

Batons out to her sides and then angled down when he could descend.

Swinging level to hold.

Only twice did she have to signal him to climb, with upraised batons.

"He's good," Ham mumbled somewhere in the background.

She, but Sly kept that to himself.

The trick was to descend until he was just above the highest point the deck ever swung. Then to be there—the exact moment it swung to its peak.

Down! Hold. Down! Hold.

He could feel the tension between them, the perfect

synchronicity of their mutual dance the moment before she gave the final signal.

Two batons straight down.

Sly shoved the collective down. If the ship was in the wrong place by so much as five feet he could pitch to the deck, shatter his rotors, maybe even be thrown overboard.

The wheels didn't even slam down onto the deck. She'd gotten him so perfectly positioned that he kissed down on it.

Following her direction, he pushed the rotor full down, creating negative lift, pinning the helo to the deck.

The disadvantage was that negative lift would drag the tips of the whirling main rotor blades dangerously low.

But he saw the deck crew scramble for the tie-downs practically on all fours. Well-rehearsed.

In less than thirty seconds, she crossed the batons in front of her chest, giving him the Cut Engines sign.

Just before she did, she held the batons out front and back, level for just an instant.

"What the hell is that sign?" Ham asked him.

"Surfin', dude. She's surfin'."

11

HAILEY TRIED TO FIGURE OUT JUST WHAT WAS HAPPENING, but couldn't seem to.

Workers Tavern was packed to the gills.

The Christmas Day wedding had been at the community pool. She supposed it made sense for the wedding of a rescue swimmer, but it was still weird to have the wedding party all in the pool and the bride and groom up on the diving board.

Weird in a gloriously small-town-funny way that she totally dug. The bride's high-brow mom hadn't looked terribly amused, but everyone else was having too much fun to care.

Hailey loved that her bikini had gobsmacked Sly Beaumont straight into stuttering silence.

Vera's shy streak wasn't doing much at fending off a whole lot of male attention. She had looked so perfect in her sleek one-piece that all the guys were hovering, including Sly's copilot.

Most of her crew had returned to the cutter. The captain had said that he wanted at least one of his AVDET people on the boat before midnight—which actually felt pretty damn good. He'd complimented them both on a difficult task well done and it felt as if they really were a part of the team already. It boded well for the five years to come.

"This is insane!" Vera had whispered as she begged off before the party shifted from the pool to the tavern.

"When you're right, you're right," Hailey had hugged her tightly g'night before following Sly to Workers for the wedding dinner and dancing. The latest deluge was so cold after the warm pool that laughter had been the only answer.

It *was* insane.

She'd known Vera and Sly for two whole weeks. And it felt as if she'd never had a closer friend or known any man better.

Now she and Sly were boogieing down to a small up-tempo band, with the four graybeards as backup vocals inventing any melodies they didn't already know—which was most of them.

The giant bartender, in an equally giant Santa suit, handed out eggnog and hearty calls of, "Ho! Ho! Ho!"

Hailey missed when she and Sly switched from dancing with the beat to... The transition from rocking out with Sylvester Beaumont to slow-dancing curled up against his chest had passed without notice. It was just so natural.

For a while, she just let herself soak in how good it felt. *He* felt. No man had ever felt this way.

And somehow it didn't surprise. Everything about Sylvester Beaumont felt easy and natural. The teasing in the bar. The perfect synchronicity during the helo's landing—he'd been masterful. Then they'd talked for hours and hours aboard the cutter despite her exhaustion, and more when they were both ashore, with flirtatious emails in between.

The twinkle lights strung from the ceiling fans... twinkled. The graybeard quartet actually found the harmony on *I Saw Mommy Kissing Santa Claus*. The laughter rippled around the bar in a slow wave while the storm raged somewhere outside in a land Hailey didn't care about at the moment.

"You thinking that you're gonna get lucky tonight, sailor?"

Hailey leaned back enough to look up into Sly's brown eyes. "Isn't that *my* line?"

Sly grinned down at her. "You weren't picking it up fast enough."

"You haven't even kissed me yet."

"Lightning," he whispered.

"What? No man has ever been this slow about kissing me before. Definitely not fast as lightning."

"Wasn't talking about that."

"What are you talking about, Surfer Boy?"

"This," and he leaned down to kiss her.

The chill of the frigid Pacific roaring outside the tavern faded away. As right as landing his helo on the pitching deck. One moment fighting the storm...

And now?

Safe on deck.

Maybe it would be her wedding next Christmas. Right here.

CAVE RESCUE COURTSHIP

Petty Officer Vera Chu *lives her dream of serving aboard a US Coast Guard cutter. When newly assigned to patrols of the treacherous Columbia River Bar, it only affirms her resolve.*

Lieutenant Hammond Markson *flies his Dolphin rescue helicopter as if it's a part of himself.*

Only when a desperate rescue on the storm-tossed Oregon Coast cliffs throws them together do they find out how truly exciting life can be.

INTRODUCTION

This is my second couple from the pilot-cutter romance in the prior story. But I wanted to explore other things in this story. Maybe it was some of that homesickness I mentioned earlier.

No, that isn't quite right.

I don't exactly *miss* the Oregon Coast, but I did love my time there very much. I mean how much rain, cold, gray, and fog can a person miss when they've moved somewhere with fifty-three more days of sun per year like Massachusetts? So, let's call it nostalgia.

I also wanted to explore more of the skills that the US Coast Guard brings to saving lives along the Oregon Coast. One of the most challenging and dangerous rescues is the cliff rescue.

The winds, after slipping undisturbed across five thousand miles of ocean, slam into the cliffs of the Oregon Coast like a battering ram. There's a story of a news team from the East Coast who had flown out to cover a post-avalanche mountain rescue on one of the

Northwest's towering dormant volcanoes. While there, a typical storm blew through at about eighty miles per hour. Suddenly all of the reports changed from mountain rescue to "The Storm of the Century." They were impressed.

On the Oregon Coast, at sixty we start paying attention. At eighty it's worth driving a car up to the cliff tops—way back from the edge—to watch the storm come in. At a hundred miles an hour, we start to hunker down and double-check that our emergency supplies are in place. At one-twenty, the anemometer on Cape Foulweather snaps off (which happened multiple times in the six years we lived just ten miles away).

A twelve-foot tide combined with a storm surge can cause major beaches to disappear underwater. Sometimes, when the storms retreat, the beaches are scoured clean down to the underlying rock. Other times, they are built up with yards-deeper sand, often stretching for miles. The Pacific Ocean thinks little of rearranging a few million tons of sand in a single event. But during the storm, it is all too easy to be trapped along these beaches with no escape—as many of the cliffs are crumbling sand, vertical sandstone, or sometimes even overhanging basalt.

Often those trapped, perhaps from a capsized fishing boat, or perhaps from wandering around a headland at low tide only to be cut off by a high one, have only one hope. Their futures are at the mercy of the only teams able to go out in even the worst storms: the US Coast Guard.

UNTITLED

Matt Buchman7,800 words
PO Box 434
Gloucester, MA 01931
matthew@mlbuchman.com
www.mlbuchman.com

Cave Rescue Courtship
by M. L. Buchman

1

"YOU ARE OFFICIALLY THE CHIEF LOON ON THIS BOAT," Petty Officer Vera Chu slid out of her upper bunk and did her best to repress a shiver. As fast as possible she stripped out of her sleeping sweats and pulled on "The Blue"—technically the ODU, Operational Dress Uniform, which sounded far too fancy for the standard Coast Guard working uniform. Blue cargo pants (over long johns), topped with a long-sleeved blue t-shirt, and blue overshirt. Her last gesture after pulling on the blue ball cap was to rub her name stitched over her right breast pocket. USCG to the core just like her parents. Dad always insisted that Mom would have been so proud of her and that was enough—almost.

"What took you so long to figure that one? I mean we've known each other like two whole weeks already." PO Hailey Beaumont mumbled from where she stayed tucked under her covers on the lower bunk.

The fifty-year-old USCG *Steadfast* wasn't exactly a warm ship, so it was hard to blame her. The cutter had a lot of quirks, but she was indeed a steadfast craft and had already proven it several times since she and Hailey had come aboard. Crossing the violent Columbia River Bar off the Oregon Coast to rescue endangered boats and their crews, the old ship had definitely proven that she still had what it took.

The two weeks had also proven that, despite any momentary lack of even implied sanity, Hailey was a good crewmate to have by your side in a tight spot.

"Perhaps I'm a slow learner. I determined you were insane last night when you returned to the ship at oh-three-hundred hours this morning singing *Little White Church.*"

Hailey pulled down the covers enough to expose her dark curly hair and one bleary eye. "I didn't. By Little Big Town?"

"You did. And yes. If you find it to be of any comfort, you were mostly on key."

She pulled the covers back over her head and Vera could barely hear her. "Who knew that country music was so dangerous?"

"Or handsome Coast Guard helicopter pilots?"

This time when Hailey emerged, she was smiling. "Okay, you got me. Sly was awesome. We slow danced until they shut down the bar. I thought you hooked up with his copilot, the dark but dashing Chief Warrant Hammond Markson. Ham left like minutes after you did. Figured you were doing the whole discreet gorgeous-Asian-chick thing."

"No." Last night had been the wedding of Sly's and Hammond's back-seat crew. The rescue swimmer and crew chief from the HH-65 Dolphin helicopter were now gone on a two-week honeymoon to Hawaii.

We're planning to swim somewhere warm for a change, the groom had announced after the wedding. Offshore Astoria, Oregon was many things, but warm ocean it wasn't. Time span to hypothermia in the summer was twelve minutes. Except this was the day after Christmas, so it was closer to four.

When the party had moved to the Workers Tavern dive bar, she'd departed to return to the ship.

"Who *did* you hook up with?" Hailey shoved aside the blankets, dumped her t-shirt to the deck, and began scrabbling through the clothes in her half of the inset drawers.

"No one." Which was technically true. She hadn't hooked up and had sex with anyone.

However, she'd glanced back at the bar after a block to spot Hammond standing outside the bar's door with his fists rammed into his jacket pockets, just watching her.

When she didn't move off, he'd come up to join her and offered to walk her back to the ship. The long, cold mile should have taken fifteen minutes. Instead it had taken most of two hours. No handholding. He hadn't even shot for a goodbye kiss. Instead he'd stood and watched until she was up the gangway, like a real gentleman.

Actually well past that. She'd peeked out from the flight deck, which was her and Hailey's domain, just making sure everything was where it should be before bunking down for the night. Hammond had still been there, a dark silhouette, still watching the gangway. He'd stood there another ten minutes before finally turning on his heel and walking back the way he'd come.

She still didn't know why the walk had taken so long, or why she hadn't been cold...until this morning. Major brrr!

"Where's the fun in not hooking up with someone after a wedding?" Hailey yanked on a doubled sports bra and a t-shirt, then kept layering up. She didn't have the decency to shiver even once.

Vera felt as if she'd been *born* cold. Only at the peak of Detroit summers had she been truly comfortable. The winters there were...harsh.

"As I said, you're a loon, Hailey. And who will you be hooking up with tonight?"

"No one but the deep sea. We're headed back out."

Vera could feel the low thrum of the idling engines vibrating through the soles of her feet against the chilly deck plates. She shifted to stand on Hailey's jeans where she'd dumped them on the floor last night. Surprise inspections were clearly not Hailey's friend.

Standing on her bunkmate's clothes probably wasn't the best form. So instead, she sat on the rumples of Hailey's vacated bunk to pull on her boots.

"But after that, Sly will be waiting for me."

Vera offered her an eye roll, but Hailey just shook her head.

"No, really. I've never just *known* a guy was a contender. Actually, I've always just known, but in the other direction—like some guy will be fun but no way more than that. This time I totally know Sly is it and that he feels the same."

"That's why you were singing *Little White Church* when you came in this morning?" Vera had never "just known" with a guy either and didn't expect to any time soon.

Hailey stopped pulling on her ODU. "*Shit!* Country music is so freaking dangerous."

Vera would take that as sound advice and stick with her Detroit fusion techno-funk.

As they headed to breakfast, the deck began swaying beneath their feet. They were off dock again and headed once more across the Colombia River Bar. Only two weeks aboard, but Vera now knew exactly what that meant: rough ride ahead.

2

"Is he always like this?" Tad called over the intercom from the back of the thrumming HH-65 Dolphin helicopter.

"No," Ham sighed. "Usually he's worse."

Lieutenant Sylvester "Sly" Beaumont sat in the right-hand pilot's seat and he was in full-on cheery Gloucester fisherman mode. Actually, that was his normal state, this was something "other" but Ham didn't want to spook their substitute rescue swimmer. With Harv and Vivian off to Hawaii—lucky sea dogs—Tad and Craig were filling in.

Seven years together flying for the Coast Guard, and he'd never seen Sly both so cheery and flying so clean. Normally Sly was a rougher pilot. Not sloppy, but more as if he was always thinking about every moment. Suddenly he was flying like it was the most natural thing in the world.

Ham couldn't imagine how else to describe it. They'd always had fun flying together, but suddenly Ham was all

Mr. Smooth and Grace, like he'd just gotten another ten years of flying skill out of nowhere.

Surely not because of some lady.

Ham knew better. He'd been Dear Hammed twice— once at the altar. Both bitches had kept the ring as well. Next time he wasn't buying the ring until *after* the goddamn wedding. Charice still wore the diamond that he'd given her, probably because her banker husband had considered it a wise saving of his Long Island capital. Hot Haitian babe and Mr. Conservative Too-goddamn-cheap New York banker, who'd have ever thought.

Evengie had hocked his second ring, along with three others he hadn't known about, and bought a ticket to Japan. The black bitch of Tokyo. Made even less sense than being a black dude in Astoria, Oregon—according to the census, there were two black families in the whole town, though he had yet to meet any of them. Hailey's and Vera's arrival had definitely raised the town's diversity.

"Winds kicking thirty, heading for forty offshore," Ham reported. A small storm by Pacific Northwest standards, but still a challenge. The clouds had rolled off the ocean in layers. Two days ago high horsetails at sunset. An overcast mid-altitude blanket yesterday. Today, low dark and nasty. It was mid-morning, but the day was so dark that even the Douglas fir woods that lay just a kilometer from the Coast Guard hangar seemed utterly featureless. Just a wall of green rather than ten thousand trees.

"Sounds good." Sly called for clearance from the Tower then signaled for Ham to take them aloft; Ham was pilot-in-command for this flight. Sly was a good captain and shared his airtime, unlike some bastards. One of the many reasons Ham liked flying with him.

Twenty-five knots of ugly slapped at their bird before they were fifty feet up. The high whine of the twin turboshaft engines deepened a little as they took up the load. The hull creaked for a moment as the load on it shifted from squatting on three wheels to dangling from its main rotor.

Sly usually loved nothing so much as grousing about flying through shitty weather—as if that wasn't a major part of their life in the two years since they were posted to Oregon.

But not today.

"Who the hell drugged you, dude?"

"Curvy little chick, totally five-by-five."

"About five-*foot*-five. Gotta be broken to see anything in you."

"You'll find out, Ham." Man couldn't even be insulted by Ham dissing his girl.

Crap! What did it take to get a rise out of him? He needed Harv and Vivian to help him straighten Sly out. Anyone talked shit about Vera Chu, and they'd find themselves looking for a new face. He glanced toward the mouth of the Columbia River and there was her boat in mid-channel, bucking over the big waves of the Bar.

He and Sly had been flying together for seven years. Suddenly, the guy's brain goes AWOL? He'd never fallen so hard, so fast. And that so wasn't what Ham himself had been doing last night standing like a doorpost off the *Steadfast's* gangway. He wasn't sure quite what he *had* been doing; he just hadn't wanted to leave. He liked being around Vera Chu.

"I'll find out what? What a fling feels like?" Not that he'd even touched Vera. She was absolutely *not* a fling sort of woman, and he and Sly were most definitely fling sort of guys. Or they had been, before Sly's libido had been attacked by a seriously cute and curvy petty officer newly assigned to the *Steadfast*.

"Nope, buddy. It's the real thing."

"Coke already has the trademark on that. Buck-fifty outta the machine; works just fine for me."

Sly just laughed.

This was gonna be a long-ass day.

3

VERA HATED THE S PART OF SAR, ESPECIALLY NEARSHORE SAR. Search-and-Rescue from aboard the Coast Guard cutter in high seas was bad enough. Out there, every spare hand was set to rotating on the watch. Often nothing showing in the chaotic waves other than a life preserver...if you were searching for one of the smarter ones. Otherwise, it might just be a floating body, less visible than a drift log in the rough waters.

She and Hailey had two typical duties: Landing Safety Officers and Gunner's Mates. With no helicopter landing on the *Steadfast's* afterdeck and no one to shoot at, SAR meant that they were issued binoculars and set to watch: two hours on, one hour off.

Near to shore, it was the same drill, except the deep ocean swell built to double the height as they became waves ready to crash on the land. Also, rather than traveling a grid pattern perpendicular to the swells, the cutter's search pattern was parallel to the coast where it was feared someone was lost.

That meant the cutter was typically broadside to the new-and-improved swells rising to crash onto the land. Black-and-blue marks were just part of the day as they were tossed against stanchions and railings like human beach balls.

They'd found a spot to brace themselves against the RB-S, the Response Boat-Small. The twenty-three-foot inflatable was stowed midships just forward of the rear flight deck that stretched half the length of the two hundred and ten-foot cutter. It gave them a spot out of the bitter wind, mostly. They could also rest their elbows on the inflatable's side tube to steady the binoculars, not that it was doing them any good.

A party of four in two double kayaks had gone missing just south of Seaside, Oregon. Reported over an hour ago, they were long dead if they were still in the water. Their only hope was if they'd made it ashore and were up in the cliffs.

"Couldn't have been north of Seaside. Oh, no," Hailey shouted loud enough to be heard over the increasing storm.

That would have been too easy. From the resort town of Seaside all the way up to Astoria, there was nothing but long sandy beaches. But the beach patrols weren't reporting any bodies. That left the cliffs to the US Coast Guard.

With ten people watching the shore, there'd already been four false alarms.

Each time, the bright orange streak of an HH-65 Dolphin would slide in to inspect the find more closely.

Each time they waved off. Flotsam tossed up on the rocks, no sign of the missing adventurers.

"Is that your boyfriend?" Vera teased Hailey to break up the monotony of the long watch in the bitter cold.

Hailey's binoculars swung aloft for a moment as the Dolphin flew slowly south on search. "Yep! That's his tail number. Looks like your boy is doing the flying today though."

"Not my boy." Despite herself, Vera swung up her binoculars to look at the helo. The copilot in the left-hand seat had his hand on the controls. Between helmet and glasses, there was little to see, but what showed of his face was far darker than the pilot's. Yes, Hammond was at the controls. The pilot in the right seat was holding binoculars of his own looking down—at them. He waved, then turned his attention back to the surf line.

Vera admonished herself and did the same. Even braced against the inflatable's hull, this was becoming hard. The powerful binoculars that let her inspect every rock, had seemed light four hours ago. Now they felt heavy as lead. And her left shoulder kept threatening to cramp. The pitching had gotten worse, and there was often green water up to the deck below theirs. Even on the lee side of the ship, they were often eating spray.

"Tide's rising," she called out to prove that she wasn't thinking about Hammond.

They'd met a couple of times over the last weeks, maybe more than that. He wasn't chatting her up, *that* she was ready for. Instead, every time there was some sort of gathering, he'd just end up near her. He was pleasant, well-educated, and well-read. In groups, he and Sly were often at the bantering center of attention. But then later she'd find the quiet, thoughtful version of him sitting quietly beside her.

"You sure?"

About Hammond? Not at all. Oh, about the tide. Vera closed her eyes as they caught another dousing. Once her eyes cleared, she checked the beach of a small cove.

"Check out the high-tide line," she told Hailey, though that wasn't how she knew. Through her binoculars, she could see that the high limit of the seaweed drift line was indeed getting caught up in the storm's wave action. It had been well above the waves when the storm started.

But Vera knew the timing because she was endlessly amazed by the huge tides here and had looked at the tide table this morning, just as she did every day.

Detroit mostly had ice and storms. Lake Erie might not kill as many as Michigan or Superior each winter, but it wasn't for lack of trying. But its tides were under two inches.

The Oregon Coast had twelve-foot tides.

Twelve-*foot* tides?

That's when Vera saw it. Not through her binoculars, but it was just as clear.

"They're not on the cliffs," Vera shouted.

"Tell me something I don't know."

"They're *in* the cliffs."

Hailey pulled aside and looked at her strangely. "I thought I was supposed to be the crazy one."

"Trust me, you are." Then Vera turned and charged down the afterdeck.

4

"THE WAY I SEE IT, HAM, YOUR BRAIN IS BROKEN."

Ham considered what it would take to dump Sly out of the helo. Release his harness, open his door, shove—hard. Yeah, totally possible.

"You seem to think that women are fun."

"Hello, duh! So did you two weeks ago."

"Seeing it all from the next level up, buddy. Next level up. Yessiree."

"Why is a Gloucester fisher-twerp suddenly talking Texas?"

"That's not Texas. That's the Duke."

"Trust me, Sly. You are so *not* John Wayne."

"You're just jealous," Sly kept scanning the surf.

"Of you, not a chance." Though he had to admit, Hailey was really something. Almost as dark as he himself was, built, sassy, and seriously amazing at her job.

"What about that Vera? You should go for her."

As if. She had some strange effect on him that he

couldn't quite get a grip on. It was like every time he got near her; he sort of lost who he was. She was all the things Hailey wasn't: quiet, elegant, and alarmingly pretty. He was never, ever tongue-tied around women. Years of cruising the bars with Sly, he'd had plenty of practice, and they could cut quite a swath with the ladies.

Not with Petty Officer Vera Chu. Her gentle dignity caught him off guard every time. Maybe if he—

"Dolphin Three-niner, this is *Steadfast.*" The radio call didn't help his thoughts, as he knew that Vera was right down there on the cutter they'd been overflying all morning.

"Go ahead, *Steadfast.*"

"I have a petty officer here with a novel theory," Chief Petty Officer Mackey's tone was as dry as the day wasn't. "Have you checked Hug Point, specifically the cave?"

He and Sly looked at each other. Two years patrolling the Oregon Coast together, and they'd never had to do a cave rescue, the worst of all SAR scenarios. Partly because the coast had only three—two local and the third over a hundred miles to the south. The last was the big Sea Lion Caves, and it had an elevator for tourists that led to the safe highway far above. The two smaller ones could be incredibly dangerous.

The cave at Hug Point seemed unlikely, because there was a fairly easy land escape nearby—the path tourists used to visit the cave in kinder weather. They'd check it first, as it was closest to them, but now he had a very bad feeling about this.

Hug Point had gotten its name back in the time of the old wagon trains. Before there were any inland routes carved through the rough Coast Range, it had been the only north-south trade road. The wagons had to literally hug the cliff even at low tide to avoid being washed out to sea.

Nosing the helo down and turning south, they reached the prominence of Hug Point in minutes. There was a waterfall, fifteen feet high and twenty-five wide, which normally made a pretty curtain. With the rush of the winter storm, the curtain was more of a shooting cannon, arcing out from the cliff in a powerful stream.

Just to the north, the surf was washing up into the sea-cave in the basalt-and-sandstone cliffs. Ham hovered as low as he dared in the turbulence where Pacific Ocean storm met steep cliff. The day was dark enough that the searchlight actually lit much of the cave's interior.

Nothing.

"Oh man," Ham really didn't like this.

Sly switched off the searchlight as Ham lifted and raced north.

There was one other cave near here, just south of Cannon Beach, inaccessible except briefly at the very lowest tides on the calmest days.

5

"No one at Hug Point," Chief Petty Officer Mackey's voice was grim.

"It was just an idea." Though Vera still felt that it had been a good one. "Sorry to have wasted your time, Chief." Hopefully he wouldn't hold it against her. Two weeks on the _Steadfast_ hadn't earned her much crazy-idea credit yet. She'd rushed onto the bridge, without being summoned, so sure that she had the solution.

Tourists were always getting into trouble at the Picture Rocks Caves on Lake Superior. A summer storm would blow up out of nowhere and slam into the beach taking a high toll among the unwary. Even all of the way down to Sector Detroit, the USCG stories of those scenic caves were told far too frequently.

"Hold your position, Petty Officer," Mackey cut off her escape.

He waved her over to the chart table where he and the captain had been conferring.

She came over and stood at the best attention she

could against the bucking ship. Thankfully, Coast Guard protocol allowed her to hang onto the table's side rail and still technically remain at attention.

"At ease, Chu. Jesus, I know you're not some first-year. Got a brain? You're not in trouble with me as long as you use it."

"Yes, Chief." She'd heard similar lines before and experience had taught her that they were trustworthy about half the time. Only two weeks aboard the *Steadfast,* she didn't yet know which side of that coin Chief Mackey landed on.

"The problem is here," he stabbed a finger at the electronic chart. It was less than five miles from their current position.

She hadn't had time to learn the coast yet, but she recognized Cannon Beach by its large sandstone sea mounts and shallow hard-basalt reefs. The chief was pointing just to the south.

"There are only two significant caves along this section of the coast. With Hug Point empty, if your guess is right, they're in a world of hurt. Silver Cave."

"What's the lay of the land there?"

"In a storm? Start with Hell. Then make it worse."

6

"YOU'RE SHITTING ME." IN TWO YEARS OF FLYING RESCUE along the Columbia Bar and a couple hundred miles of seashore to the north and south, Ham had never had occasion to come so close to Silver Cave.

Though the cove lay just south of the resort town of Cannon Beach, it was almost wholly inaccessible. The cliffs offered no landside entry, and the sea was filled with boat-ripping rocks. On a calm day, it was a beautiful place. Steep cliffs over a hidden beach. Sometimes there was sand, but in the winter the beach was big cobbles and rocks.

Just off the jagged point, a small sea mount had been cut off from the land. It sat prettily, like the period on an exclamation point. Tenacious conifers formed a small green crown on the hard rock.

At low tide, it was connected to the land by a wash of seaweed-shrouded boulders and tide pools. At high tide, it became an island.

In a storm?

"You're shitting me," Sly echoed his comment.

The deep ocean swell hit the shallows in twenty-foot surf that shattered against the back of the small sea mount. The passage between the mount and the land was a thrash of crossing currents that had slammed around either side of mount to smash against each other when they met on the far side.

Clouds of spray and confused whitewater breakers filled the intervening area with chop tall enough to bury a helicopter without even noticing.

And on the landside of the sea mount, facing the inaccessible cliff rather than the sea, was Silver Cave. It had been carved into the back side of the hard point of the sea mount that had withstood the waves.

"Winds at thirty, north-northwest. Gusting thirty-five."

Ham really wished it hadn't been his turn as pilot-in-command. But, because Sly was a stickler as well as being a good guy, unless the flight dragged on too long and fatigue became a factor, it was Ham's flight for the duration.

"Call the cliff," he instructed Sly.

"Roger."

A Dolphin HH-65's rotor was forty feet across. The distance from cliff to cave was six times that, but in this wind, he wanted an extra set of eyes on it.

He came in high, but there was nothing to see.

Easing down, he kept his nose into the wind to get the least buffeting from each gust. That northwest wind turned them so that Sly faced mostly toward the cliff. He began calling distances.

Ham eased down into the slot.

"I've got some color," Tad called out from the rear.

"See it." Please let it just be a fisherman's float.

Bright blue. Then yellow.

Then...

Two double kayaks, one snapped in half, came into view. They'd been dragged partway into the cave.

He eased down another ten feet to get a better angle on the cave.

There was still a body in one of the seats.

But its head was impossibly far forward, and it wasn't moving.

A face peeked out from deeper within the cave.

Someone waved at them desperately, then was almost dragged out to sea as the surf washed into the cave's mouth. He'd be a goner except that the cave's floor sloped up to the rear.

"Got a live one," he and Tad called simultaneously.

7

VERA LOOKED AT THE VIDEO FEED FROM THE HELO. EVEN Lake Michigan never created a mess like this one.

There was nowhere to drop the rescue swimmer that he wouldn't be immediately killed against the massive boulders. Lowering him in by a winch would still drop him in the surf that the boulders were churning into a maelstrom.

Vera checked her watch. "This tide has another six feet of rise."

"That's a death certificate," Mackey acknowledged.

The captain was already underway toward the sea mount, not that there was anything a cutter could do there.

Even a small boat...

"Uh, Chief? No never mind." It was too stupid for words. No crazy-idea credits in the world would cover this one. But the image stuck in her mind.

"Spit it out, Vera." She was surprised he even knew her first name.

Even after the Captain approved it ten minutes later, she still knew it was the craziest idea of her life.

"One more thing, sir?"

The captain nodded at her as he studied the detailed chart to see how close he could get to the shore.

"Request permission to volunteer, sir."

That snagged his full attention.

"If someone else went, and this doesn't work..."

He studied her intently and she didn't flinch.

Finally he nodded. "Do the Guard proud." Then he turned to confer with the navigator.

She scrambled aft to get ready. She'd just gone from crazy to stupid. Hopefully she wouldn't go to dead.

8

Ham hovered twenty feet above the wavetops while Craig lowered Tad, their rescue swimmer, down on the helicopter's winch cable.

He couldn't see what was beneath him, so Craig the crew chief was calling out positioning moves. "Five back. Hold. Up ten. Hold."

The litany had been practiced too many times for it to fully occupy his thoughts, though he wished it did.

He'd been called back to the ship just as the Response Boat-Small was lowered into the water by the cutter. He couldn't carry the RB-S, they'd need a JayHawk for that, but there wasn't one available for another hour, and that might be too late.

But that wasn't the heartstopper. *That* happened when Ham saw one of the RB-S's occupants. No one, but no one moved like Petty Officer Vera Chu. Her elegance showed in every gesture, even fighting to help the coxswain get the boat launched. It had been impressed on his very eyeballs since the first moment he saw her.

Too dumbfounded to speak, he'd slid to hover over the pitching rubber boat.

"What the hell is she doing there?" He couldn't keep it in any longer.

"Who?" Craig asked from the back. "Left ten."

"No way. That was her?" Sly tried to look down at the RB-S through the nose window by their feet.

"Swimmer in the boat," Craig announced. "And... we're hooked to the RB-S. Up ten, I'm spooling cable. Up ten more."

Ham lifted the helo even as his heart sunk.

9

"YOU CRAZY, SISTER?"

"Asks the rescue swimmer," Vera chided him. They were the ultimate warrior in the Coast Guard hierarchy, jumping out of helos to rescue desperate people from fast-sinking boats. She'd never seen him before. He must be the substitute for Harvey now on his honeymoon.

"Hey, I'm paid to be crazy. You're doing that all on your own. I like that in a Guardsman."

"Guardswoman." Vera wore a full float suit, unlike the diver who wore a dry suit. If she hit the water, she'd float like a balloon animal; he needed to be able to swim and dive. They were both International Orange for maximum visibility.

Like a lot of swimmers, he was a big guy. His broad shoulders and well-muscled legs were obvious even through his suit. Which had her looking aloft.

Hammond was up there. Just fifty feet away. And he was now her lifeline.

Literally.

Here was her crazy idea come to life. A Dolphin helo —too small to wholly lift an RB-S—could, however, offer stabilization. With the two big engines removed and a small one in their place, the helo could even loft the boat briefly between the worst troughs, hopefully keeping its bottom off the submerged reef. Most importantly, its three-point lifting harness that had been rigged onto the boat should keep it upright.

The rubber tube sides of the boat itself would hopefully protect them when they would be inevitably slammed sideways into rocks.

At least that was the image in her head.

10

"You okay, Ham?"

"Why wouldn't he be okay?" Craig, the substitute crew chief, jumped on Sly's question like an attack dog.

"Because that's his girlfriend down there. So shut up a minute."

Ham looked down, not that there was anything to see. The RB-S was beneath and slightly behind them as he dragged it toward the coast. The only thing visible was the churning surf he was now dragging her into.

Petty Officer Vera Chu wasn't his girlfriend. All they'd ever done was sat and talked. Sly and Hailey would be off cracking jokes in the middle of a crowd or dancing in the limited space between the tables at the Workers Tavern. He and Vera would be talking about their Coast Guard pasts.

Last night, walking her home, he found out that they'd both lost a parent to the Iraq War: his Air Force father, her Coast Guard mother. He'd also learned that, like him, she was committed to the Coast Guard until they retired them or were carried out feet first. Her pride of being a third generation Coastie shone in every word she spoke about following in her mother's footsteps.

He'd never liked anyone as much...not even women he'd slept with.

And here he was dragging her into one of those situations that could end with her broken or dead all too easily.

Suddenly he was so glad he was the pilot-in-command. Because if anyone was going to protect her dream, it was damn well going to be him.

"I got this," he told Sly, then eased up on the collective enough to feel the strain on the winch cable and started the race for the beach.

11

Something had changed.

Vera could feel the Dolphin hesitating, hanging there above them as the RB-S rode up and down the big ocean swell close behind the first line of breakers.

Suddenly, their boat was being dragged forward, riding the back of a wave at exactly the same speed as the water. It was a good move. When the wave broke, they'd be able to ride the leading edge of the trough...the deepest water that wasn't under a breaker.

"You're watching that helo hard enough to make a man jealous, sister," the rescue swimmer was teasing her again.

"That's my man up there." She didn't know why she said it. The change in control had probably been Sly taking command from Hammond, which meant that was Hailey's man doing the flying up there. But she didn't care.

"Shit. Why are the hot ones always taken?" He made

it sound like a compliment and tease rather than grumpy and chauvinistic.

"Guess I'm just lucky."

He snorted a laugh then turned his attention to the fast approaching sea mount. Suddenly he was all business. "You ready?" he shouted at the coxswain sitting back by the small engine. He nodded rather than trying to shout against the rain and wind.

"All you two have to do is get this boat nosed as far into the cave as you can. I'll be off before the second wave breaks. My goal is to load one person between each breaker and be out of there by the fifth wave. I figure that's about four times longer than our luck is likely to hold and I get itchy when I push my luck by more than a factor of ten. So, we aren't gonna go there. Clear?"

"Clear."

The crest before them started to shatter. She sat in the frontmost seat, where the gunner's mate would normally sit when an M2 .50 cal machine gun would be on the forward swivel mount. She felt a little naked with no gun and just a bow rope in her hands.

The seat itself was like a narrow horse saddle without stirrups. The horn and cantle were curved bars to provide secure handholds fore and aft. She could clamp her knees on the side and still have both feet firmly on the deck. It allowed her to sway back and forth like a bronc rider as the RB-S slammed through the waves.

Her nerves were moving faster than the waves though.

"You think this is going to work?" Vera shouted to the

swimmer though he sat just in the next seat back and to the side.

"Crazy as shit, but it's the best chance these people have. If we survive, I'm gonna have to shake the hand of whatever crazy bastard thought this up."

"Why wait?" She held out her hand. "And that would be crazy bitch." She didn't know what had come over her, but she liked the way it felt.

He shook her hand hard and grinned before nodding aloft. "Does he know how goddamn lucky he is?"

She didn't know. But if they lived through this, she was certainly going ask.

12

HAM REALLY WISHED HE SURFED. HE'D SAVED ENOUGH surfers over the years, and failed to save a few others, that there wasn't a chance they'd ever get him out on a board. But knowing the waves better would be really useful at the moment.

"Twelve-thirty!" Sly called out and held out a fist aimed close ahead and just to the right.

The trough immediately ahead of their wave dipped down to reveal a massive boulder.

Ham swung left, hoping he'd drag the RB-S sideways in time. They'd have no vision ahead and had to trust the flight crew. Because of the long lead on the winch line, he had to judge the lag time in guiding them.

"And—" Sly didn't even have time to point.

"Got it." Ham slalomed them back the other way. The deeper channel was darker blue, and he began following it.

"Sea mount in ten." Sly fed him information he didn't have time to think about for himself.

The approach was going to be hard on the boat. The rocks in front of the cave were barely awash in the troughs and were buried in twenty feet of spray and crashing surf when the waves met coming around either side of the mount.

He rode the curl of the wave, carving a path to the front of the sea cave.

That's when he saw the problem.

"Winch out! Winch out! Emergency!"

"Paying out cable," Craig replied, and the high whine of the winch motor sounded in the cabin.

As it paid out, Ham climbed, but held his turn.

Just as the surf slapped against itself and died back, he had the RB-S lined up at the front of the cave. With the cable now pressed into the protruding upper lip of the cave, the plan had been for him to descend. That would provide enough slack, as the RB-S used their small motor to power forward, to drive up into the cave.

"Keep running the cable?" Craig called over the intercom.

"Uh, yes please."

He and Sly were both pressed back as hard as they could be in their seats.

The long nose of the Dolphin was rested against the rock slope of the top of the sea mount. Beyond that stood a tiny clump of coastal pine: stout, twisted, and wind-blown so their crowns leaned dramatically back toward the land. Their trunks were thick with age and surviving ten thousand storms.

The rotor blades were spinning an arc mere feet from the miniature grove atop the sea mount.

13

VERA SPOTTED THREE SURVIVORS HUDDLED AT THE VERY highest point in the back of the small cave. One broken arm. One head wound. One walking on an ankle that twisted sideways, but clearly hadn't realized it yet. The fourth one and the two parts of kayaks reported by the helo crew must have been washed out to sea.

The second wave slashed into the boat on the swimmer's heels as he jumped forward into the cave. Thankfully, the cave's bottom had been carved so that it rose toward the back. But green water flowed over the rear transom and partially swamped their twenty-three-foot boat.

Vera managed to loop the bow line over a barnacle-covered boulder and calculated desperately as she held on.

They already had water aboard: six feet wide, half a foot deep, twenty-three feet long. Sixty cubic feet, approximately five hundred gallons, or...four thousand pounds. The useful payload on the Dolphin HH-65 was under fifteen hundred.

True to his word, the swimmer had the first survivor aboard before the next wave rushed into the small cave. His arm hung ghoulishly askew. The coxswain came forward and tucked the man's wrist into the front of his life vest to immobilize it.

The boat wouldn't sink when filled with water, not even with great gouges ripped in the hull. But it was a sure bet that the helicopter couldn't tow them back out through the heavy surf.

The guy walking on the side of his foot managed to collapse into the boat after wave number three.

The small boat engine would be no help. The coxswain had run it at full thrust to drive them as far into the cave as possible. As expected, that had meant running it hard over the rocks and it would never function again without a new propeller and drive shaft.

The third wave washed up and down the length of the boat.

The rescue swimmer, there hadn't even been a chance to find out his name, was doing some emergency first aid on the head wound.

Vera watched, mesmerized for a moment, as he bound the woman's scalp back onto her head with quick loops of gauze.

They were relatively safe in the cave for the moment, but they couldn't leave.

Removing the rear transom to drain the boat was an option, but not a good one. They'd still have to be dragged through the impossible surf.

If only they could lift off the top of the cave as neatly as the woman's scalp had been lifted away.

Vera looked at the slender winch cable and let out a bark of a laugh.

14

SLY THUMPED HIS BEER MUG LOUDLY ON THE TABLE AS HE rose to his feet.

The Workers Tavern was packed and the Coasties had snagged the last table by arriving early. It was clearly the hot spot among local dive bars for getting your lady a steak dinner on Valentine's Day.

"Six weeks ago, Petty Officer Chu kicked some serious ass," he announced in a voice loud enough to get the whole bar's attention. Or it would have been in any normal bar. At Workers, loud proclamations were no reason to pay any particular attention.

The four old graybeards at their usual spot along the back leg of the U-shaped bar were seriously off melody with the Frankie Valli tune *Sherry* pumping out of the old jukebox. The laughter and chatter at other tables didn't abate in the least as Sly continued.

"The US Coast Guard has been right generous with their medals for our little escapades."

Ham figured that was why Sly had insisted that they

all wear their dress whites, specifically so that he could show off his medal to his fiancée Hailey.

"And no one deserves it more, well, other than me—"

Hailey's snort of laughter should have put him in his place.

Instead he said, "Excuse me for a second," and gave her a kiss long enough to leave her looking a little dreamy. "Now, where was I?"

"Busy congratulating yourself," Tad and Craig said in unison. They were now permanent fixtures on the crew. Harvey and Vivian had been recruited by Station Maui while they were honeymooning there.

"No, that's not it." He made a show of patting his pockets as if looking for what he'd forgotten, but his grin said that he hadn't for a moment.

Ham looked at Vera and they shared a smile. Over the two months since her arrival, she'd come to know Sly's antics as well as he did. Of course the four of them were rarely apart when the girls were ashore or the helo was aboard the *Steadfast*.

"Oh, here it is." Sly held up an imaginary bit of paper and squinted at it before continuing. "To the, highly decorated I might add, Petty Officer Chu for thinking up and executing a rescue that even my Hailey said was too crazy for her."

"You've definitely got the 'Chief Loon' award on this team," Hailey announced. In fact, she held up a funky handmade medal that was a fingernail polish-painted duckish bird, dangling from an ocean-blue ribbon. She leaned over and pinned it next to Vera's Coast Guard Medal.

Vera actually blushed, which was pretty damn cute.

"And to Lieutenant Hammond Markson," Sly paused dramatically, "the only pilot I know good enough to have pulled it off without getting us all killed. Hear! Hear!" Sly called out.

And at that, the whole bar raised their glasses and repeated the call.

Now Ham could feel the heat on his own face.

15

"YOU AREN'T SAYING MUCH." VERA DIDN'T KNOW WHY THAT was making her nervous. She and Hammond had sat with the others for hours, reliving the Silver Cave rescue, among others.

Unable to remove the top of the cave, and knowing the boat would never leave the cave intact, Vera had the helicopter back off from the cave's mouth.

Disconnecting the winch's cargo hook from the boat, she'd tied a rope line just above the hook. One by one, they attached the survivors to the cable. Then, they'd eased the line until the person swung off the boat and sideways out of the cave, but clear of the heavy surf. Once they were winched aloft, the helo lowered the cargo hook again, and they'd pulled it back into the cave with the line. A right-angle rescue; out *then* up.

One by one, everyone had gone aloft until only she and the swimmer had been left in the boat inside the cave.

"Seriously, lady. Your pilot doesn't wise up, I call first

dibs." And that's how she was finally introduced to Tad, waiting for the cable to lower back down to fetch her.

Tonight, Hammond, who usually let her know his thoughts, was keeping them very firmly to himself.

The last six weeks had been the best weeks of her life. The captain and Chief Mackey had made it clear that she was welcome to bring any crazy idea to their attention at any time of day or night. And they'd said it enough times that she actually believed them. And when the inevitable publicity had happened, neither had taken any of the credit. Instead, they'd made a point of pushing her, Tad, and Hammond to the fore.

"We aren't the ones who did it, Chu. Now take your goddamn bow." Mackey had grumbled in what she was learning was his especially pleased tone. She'd also taken the promotion that went along with the medal.

"Vera."

Hammond didn't make it a question as he stopped at the base of the *Steadfast's* gangway. All she could do was nod against a dry throat.

He reached out and took her hand, something he almost never did in public, and rubbed his thumb over the back of her knuckles, leaving a line of warmth that didn't fade away. But still he didn't speak.

"Hammond."

He shook his head. "I had all these words. Now I can't remember any of them."

"What were they about?"

He opened his mouth, closed it again.

Then he started to kneel. While it wasn't raining at the moment, the pavement was wet and muddy.

"No, Hammond. Your dress whites." At least those were the words that came out of her mouth. Her thoughts were suddenly very silent as if waiting.

Hammond stood back upright, but he was now holding open a white box which held a ring with a sapphire-blue diamond.

"The color of the sea."

He just nodded. "Yeah. That was part of the words I had. It's in your blood and I love that about you."

She didn't need any other words. Instead she held out her hand for him to slip on the ring. Then she wrapped her arms around him and held on.

That's what she loved about him too.

There was a little tune running through the back of her mind as Hammond held her tighter. It took her a moment to identify it; then couldn't help smiling even more when she did.

Hailey was going to laugh herself sick.

It was *Little White Church* by Little Big Town.

LIFEBOAT LOVE

*After failing to land themselves Coast Guard husbands, **local women Tabby and Suzy** set off from Astoria, Oregon to find a future of their own making.*

*   **Rescue Swimmer Tad** and his **rescue-helo Crew Chief Craig** have been playing the field together at the bars for years.*

*   But when the two local women, now turned Coast Guard lifeboat drivers, show up in town, all roaming thoughts are soon lost at sea—target acquired.*

INTRODUCTION

These stories have led me in a circle. I never know quite why this happens.

Sometimes, like my Delta Force and Night Stalkers stories, they just keep leading me on. Others, like my three firefighting short story series: Hotshots, Fire Lookouts, and Firebirds, I'm led full circle in a set of five stories. Occasionally, I'm fooled into thinking I've written all of a world that I intend to, but another story (sometimes years later) will raise its hand and begin calling for words to be put on the page.

For the moment at least, it feels as if this circle of tales is complete.

The fifth (and last?) story in my US Coast Guard series came about from my desire to return to multiple threads from the earlier stories.

I'm a technical guy, obviously, and I love writing about the amazing tools and techniques used by many of my characters, from television kitchens in the Dead Chef series to plane-crash investigations in the Miranda Chase series.

But what I *really* love writing about is the people.

And tickling away in the back of my mind were the two nameless women from Astoria, Oregon itself. In *Flying Beyond the Bar* they were flirting hot and heavy with my helo pilots in hopes of getting a wedding ring from a US Coast Guard officer.

I grew up in small towns, one of just twelve hundred people. And in writing those two women, I got to thinking about Wendy.

She was a grown-up and wise sixteen, I was twelve—her high school to my elementary school. We were both fans of the school's soccer team; I was a ball boy and, in retrospect, I realize she was dating Brad, one of my favorite players. But she was always funny, had a laugh for all my bumbling ways (I wasn't at all athletic, I just liked the team), and, as we stood shivering together on the chilly sidelines, she'd often joke about how we'd marry and run away together once we both graduated. She was one of the major older-woman crushes of my childhood, even though we moved away the next year.

I suspect that like most women in that town, she married a local boy and has lived out her life on a farm there. I hope it was a happy life because she was one of the most innately kind people I've ever met.

Anyway, these two women flirting in the Workers Tavern made perfect sense to me. In a small town, a glimmer of someone special would shine like gold.

Then in *Christmas Over the Bar* I needed to sweep

them offstage so that my pilots could fall for my new crew members aboard the USCG Cutter *Steadfast*.

But I didn't just let them drop away. Instead, I had another character tell them that they had to go out into the world to discover what they really wanted, what they really deserved. As I wrote subsequent stories, I kept being curious about what they learned. Perhaps for Wendy's sake.

Added to that, I wanted to revisit both my motor lifeboat from the first story and my rescue swimmer from the second. Those are both truly amazing roles that exemplify the very best of the US Coast Guard to my mind.

First, I called up a new rescue swimmer.

A year had passed since I wrote that earlier story, so second, I brought the two girls home, having now become much wiser women.

And that created the core of *Lifeboat Love*.

UNTITLED

Matt Buchman7800 words
PO Box 434
Gloucester, MA 01931
matthew@mlbuchman.com
www.mlbuchman.com

Lifeboat Love

by M. L. Buchman

1

"THERE'S SOMETHING WRONG WITH THESE PEOPLE," CRAIG waved his sandwich at the rest of the table.

"Says the dude eating a clubhouse like the pansy he is." Tad held up his own monstrous Buschman Burger, dripping with mushrooms, onions, and cheese out every side to make his point. The Workers Tavern was crowded with locals and off-duty Coasties, and most of them, Tad was glad to see, ate real food—not little triangular sandwiches on white toast.

The USCG Station Cape Disappointment and its Motor Lifeboat School were just over the big bridge in Ilwaco, Washington. And the rescue helos of USCG Sector Columbia River were planted at the Astoria, Oregon airport on this side. There were also a pair of two-hundred-and-ten-foot cutters perched at the Astoria docks when they weren't out saving people's asses.

Meeting in the middle at Workers, nestled under the big bridge that crossed the four-mile width of the mouth of the Columbia River was a thing long before he and Craig had shown up.

"Just shows I've got taste." Craig grimaced at Tad's burger. It was an argument that had gone back to their third day of deployment together four years ago and they'd joyfully never resolved it.

"Just shows you're a lazy crew chief, sitting on your ass in the helo, while us swimmers do the real work."

"Fine, next time I won't haul you back out of the ocean after a rescue and you may content yourself with swimming home."

Tad decided he was too hungry to keep it going, so he took a big bite of his burger before he remembered Craig's comment and looked around their table. "*Whuf* ifz rong mif deez people?" he managed.

Craig rolled his eyes, then waved at the two couples sharing their table.

The cutter *Steadfast* was in to dock so Hailey and Vera, the two Landing Safety Officers, were ashore. And they sat with their helo-pilot husbands. It wouldn't be quite so irksome if they weren't all happier'n roosters-in-the-henhouse about it. *And* it was just rotten luck that they were the two pilots for his and Craig's rescue helo.

Sly and Ham just never shut up about these two women. Which was nauseating...except it wasn't.

He'd liked Vera when they did a cave rescue together. Hot, funny, but with an elegance that looked amazing on her. And Hailey was a hell of a laugh. The four of them actually made it look as if happy-ever-after existed.

Tad scanned the dive bar.

It looked the same as always. Battered as a twenty-year-old manure spreader. The only reason it didn't collapse into the river and wash away was because it lay a block back from the waterfront. The late afternoon June sunlight sparkled off the sea salt that had been washed off from March's final storm. The light was out there, it just didn't dare come inside which gave the place a muddy but comfortable feel.

Beer and booze signs on three walls; the fourth was covered in small bills from a hundred or more countries —for almost a hundred years mariners had been filling in the gaps on that wall of Workers Tavern.

The big U-shaped bar took up half the space. Four old graybeards, too aged to go out to sea, sat in their usual spot telling lies and singing off-key harmonies to the jukebox. The tiny kitchen in the back offered the best meat in town. And the scattering of tables looked just as work-worn as the graybeards.

But the bar looked different in some way.

Normally when he scanned it, he'd see if there were any likely women about. Charlene was in, but she already had some boy-o at her side. She was fun, but not enough to get upset about. There was a new pair of fairly hot chicks he hadn't seen before, but he'd spotted them holding hands when they came in, and were now very cozy at the bar. Nothing happening there.

Tonight though, it all looked just a little *too* familiar. All the training time and hard work, yet all he'd done was trade one small town for another. Not a chance was he going to find what the Coasties sitting at his table seemed to have in spades. Of course, they hadn't fallen for local talent: these Coasties had married Coasties. Local talent was *always* a bad bet.

Didn't matter. He'd never wanted that cute-couple stamp anyway.

But...they did make it *look* damn tasty.

Maybe he'd better stick with harassing Craig and eating his Buschman Burger. At least those he understood.

2

"YOU READY FOR THIS?" SUZY GRIPPED THE RUSTED DOOR handle of Workers Tavern.

"So not. It looks even worse than the last time we were here. What delusion makes you think I want to do this?" Tabby Alton would rather throw herself off the pier. Of course, it was June, so it wouldn't be that much of a hardship—until the Columbia's fierce current swept her out to sea.

"You remember what Marj Kaye used to say."

Tabby sighed. No need to make it a question because of course she did.

They spoke in unison. "You've got to face your *shit* and move on." Their third-grade teacher never would have deigned to say "shit" of course, but all of the kids had picked it up that way as soon as Suzy had modified it.

"But why?" Tabby waved a hand at the tavern. It was a dark hole under the on-ramp to the soaring Astoria-Megler suspension bridge. A place filled with memories of who they *used* to be. How many nights had they come

here in tight tank tops to troll for a USCG husband? Way
too many.

"Because," Suzy swung open the door. Seared meat,
spilled beer, and off-key music reeled drunkenly out onto
the sidewalk, stumbling on the cracks. "I'm hoping that
Vivian is here. I'd like to thank her."

"Oh, okay." That was good. She'd thought it might be
one of her best friend's long-running guy quests that she
was inevitably swept up in.

A year ago they'd been majorly chatting up a pair of
Coastie officers right here in Workers—best chance at
getting out that an Astoria girl could have. Then a female
petty officer had nudged her way onto *their* table, busting
up the play but good. The guys left. PO Vivian Schroder
had delivered a lecture on all that it took to escape a town
was *leaving.* And that until they'd looked around the
outside world for themselves, they'd never know what
they really wanted, or deserved.

Vivian had been hella persuasive. She made it all
sound so real and possible. So they'd gone. Bus to
Portland, then Suzy's whim had led them south. They'd
ended up frying donuts in a hole in Alameda called Lee's.
It wasn't really a hole; it was just another place in another
strip mall in an upscale neighborhood close to the water
—though a step down from the Blue Scorcher back home
—the best bakery in Astoria.

She'd been the one who'd walked into the Coast
Guard Recruiting office on the other side of the building
from Lee's. Maybe it had been a fit of nostalgia for
Astoria. Or maybe just wanting to see an eligible male
not stuffing his waistline with lemon-filled carbs soaked

in sugar, then glazed, then topped with sprinkles. Even the sight of a sprinkle had made her nauseous since then. Neither one of them ended up dating the recruiter, but they'd walked out of the office signed up to serve.

Weirdly, training had suited both of them down to their boots. When it came time to file a Station preference, it had barely taken a glance at each other before they both wrote Astoria in the blank.

Steppenwolf's *Magic Carpet Ride* wandered out the door and thankfully faded fast into sunset—gone before the second verse.

"I wonder if Sly and Ham are still here?" Suzy remarked before breezing through the door to Workers Tavern.

"I *knew* it!" But Tabby was standing outside talking to herself. She hadn't even remembered their names, but Suzy never forgot a guy. She was like a flirt-savant.

Resigned to her doom, Tabby stepped out of the bright light of the long evening into near darkness of the tavern. She ran into Suzy's back and almost knocked her to the floor.

"What?"

"They *are* here."

"Where?" She followed the angle of Suzy's head; ever since kindergarten it was the very best indicator of where the cute guys were.

She recognized them easily. Ham dark as night and Sly looking like he'd last sunbathed, maybe, in a former life. She'd remembered them as so dashing and so much larger than life.

They still were pretty dashing, but they appeared to

be more human-sized. She and Suzy were Coast Guardswomen now, so it brought the two officers into somewhat sharper focus. Sure they were just E-3 grade Seaman, but E-4 Petty Officer Third Class was looming near, if they did well on their first real assignment.

But Sly and Ham were already sitting next to two women, also clearly in the Guard. There was just something about how a trained sailor sat that said they weren't locals.

She also noticed the two other men at the table. The one with his back to her had the unmistakable shoulders of a rescue swimmer, and he wasn't Harvey.

"Vivian's gone." A different swimmer and crew chief now sat to Ham's and Sly's other side from the women.

"Aw shit. Maybe they'll know where she went." And Suzy just walked right up to the table. Nothing about socially awkward, or time to turn tail and run. They'd both been more than willing to bed the two pilots on the off chance of getting a ring from them. And they'd all four known those terms.

She spotted the sparkler on each of the women's hands. Yep! Married. The two Guardswomen had pulled off what she and Suzy hadn't been able to—even if she and Suzy had been doing it for all the wrong reasons.

"Hey Sly. Hi Ham." Suzy planted herself at the end of the table by the two new guys. "Is Vivian still around?"

Sly looked over and called out cheerily, "Hey Suzy! Long time no see." Because he was just as unflappable as Suzy.

Ham looked up, first at Suzy, then at her. It took him a moment, then he blinked hard. His expression clearly said that if his skin had been lighter it would be shining red with a blush.

"Naw! She and Harvey shipped out to Hawaii for their honeymoon and never came back."

Tabby could feel the blood drain from her face.

Ham spoke softly. "Not dead. They signed up over there. Warm water rescuer."

"Yeah, left the cold shit to me." The swimmer, who still had his back to her, said with deep chagrin and a bit of humor.

3

TAD COULD FEEL SOMETHING. THE SWIMMER'S ITCH. AT sea, a swimmer never knew what they'd encounter during a rescue and had to develop "ten-eighty" awareness.

The best swimmer he'd ever met, Senior Chief Vernon, had insisted that knowing three-sixty degrees around you in water wasn't enough. A collapsing mast could come from above, the lash of a snapping line from behind, a shark from below, and a wave from any damn direction it was in the mood for.

"Three-sixty around, three-sixty over, and three-sixty under. One-thousand-and-eighty-degree awareness at all times. Forget about a single slice of that ten-eighty and it *will* get you. You know what happens then?"

"You die, Senior Chief," had been his naive answer.

"No, you idiot. The people depending on you to rescue them die. That's a thousand times worse. Got it, Meat?" He'd called all swimmer hopefuls that. Just meat for the grinder that was swimmer school and its eighty percent failure rate.

"Yes, Senior Chief."

Then ten minutes later Vernon would prove that Tad didn't have a clue, again.

The proudest day of his life hadn't been making it to rescue swimmer. It had been the Senior Chief shaking his hand after graduation. "Go make us proud, Swimmer."

Tad knew no higher praise.

And right now, his swimmer's itch—another of Vernon's phrases—was itching something fierce.

Sparky brunette beside him. Excellent breasts under a Coastie-blue tee, right at eye-level as he was sitting, so he let himself enjoy the view for a moment before looking farther afield. Face was no disappointment. You could just tell she had a sass-factor set to permanent high. Even so, rigidly posted in an "at ease" stance, she stood like a first-year addressing officers on base. It always took them a while to chill in public.

At the bar, the old guys were swaying their way through the Beatles' *When I'm Sixty-four,* an age they'd abandoned decades before. That the Stones were rocking *Wild Horses* on the juke didn't seem to faze them. Grandma had always been a hardcore Beatles' fan. *None of those upstart Stones in my house.* Because he landed on her side of the duplex every day after school, he knew all thirteen core albums by heart. Grandma wasn't one for remixes and US re-releases.

Sly was grinning up at the lady attached to the nice breasts. The two of them were tossing it back and forth like it was old times. At least until Hailey fisted him pretty hard in the ribs.

Vera had no need to tap Ham; he was looking thoroughly embarrassed. Had they both dallied with Ms. Breasts and now...

No, Ham wasn't looking at the sparky brunette but rather behind Tad's back.

He glanced around.

Then he fully turned to get a better view.

Cut from the same cloth, yet totally different. The quiet blonde was a study. Built just like her brunette pal, the same five-eight and fit-as-hell. Maybe a little more in the shoulder. But his gaze didn't even hesitate at her chest despite the same tight blue t-shirt. Her face and piercing blue eyes were far too arresting to waste time looking anywhere else.

"Ma'am," he greeted her respectfully enough to earn him a surprised laugh from Craig. The blonde was the sort to command respect.

She arched a single eyebrow.

"Grandma had that down." He touched his own forehead and pulled up his right eyebrow. "Scary as shit lady, I can tell you."

"And you loved her very much," the blonde said softly.

Tad didn't know that it was so obvious, but he shrugged its truth.

"Mine too. Grannie is awesome. And I was terrified of her every time I screwed up. Still am, I suppose."

Tad could just imagine Ms. Blonde being a scary grandma herself someday. Real easy to imagine.

4

"STILL SORRY WE CAME HOME?"

"Wrong time to ask." Tabby stared at the bilge of the forty-seven-foot Motor Lifeboat, 47-MLB, that they'd just spent two hours contorting themselves worse than a yoga class to scrub down. The bilge, the very bottom of the boat, sparkled. And every bit of grime, grease, and she didn't want to know what, was now embedded in her skin.

"I'm talking about the boys."

"You always are." Last night at Workers, everyone had squeezed over and they'd found one spare chair. She and Suzy had shared it, one cheek each. Suzy had spent the whole evening prodding at Craig's cultured Long Island, New York bonhomie. She and Tad had discussed grandmothers. His passed away three years back, hers still tenacious as could be, living alone out on the sandy, windswept side of Warrenton, Oregon. *House I was married in. House I'll die in.*

Tad had laughed. "Adair, Iowa. Not the sort of place

folks leave much. Excepting anyone who can figure a way out."

"Astoria, Oregon. Place I thought I'd never want to come back to."

She'd liked his easy laughter at himself. And despite all of his teasing of Craig, it was clear that he trusted him as only a rescue swimmer could trust his helo crew chief. Tad's life often truly depended on Craig just as much as others' lives depended on Tad going in the water.

But she and Suzy were assigned to the motor lifeboats on the other side of the Columbia River from the airport. They'd both chosen boat operations and there was no better berth they could have drawn. The Motor Lifeboat School, located at the Cape Disappointment Station— Cape D—on the Columbia River was the most prestigious school of its type in the world.

Suzy had taken her dad's penchant for being the town's best car mechanic straight into the engine room. Her own target, Boatswain's Mate, was going to be a long road before she could con her own boat. Senior Chief McAllister had made that clear when he'd assigned her to Sarah Goodwin's boat. And BM First Class, BM1, Sarah Goodwin had assigned her to help Suzy clean the bilge.

"A BM knows every inch of her boat and every skill of her crew."

Then she'd turned away as if neither of them existed. Now they crouched exhausted to either side of the immaculate twin Detroit diesel engines.

A voice came through the access hatch above. "You sure you know which side of the scrub brush cleans things up? Boat looks fine. But damn, girl."

Tabby looked up to see BM1 Sarah Goodwin smiling down at her.

Then the smile clicked off. "Five more just like her along the dock. Don't take so long this time."

Tabby stared down at the fouled water in her pail and considered throwing herself into it. Ugly way to drown, but still...six?

By the time they finished the other five boats, even Suzy wasn't wasting energy talking about guys.

5

TAD TRIED TO THINK OF HOW TO BRING IT UP WITHOUT quite bringing it up. "Haven't seen much of the girls lately." Okay, subtle was never his best play. *Subtle as a bull in heat,* Paw had always said of him all the way back to T-ball days. Tad had ruled first base, *the* hot spot in T-ball.

"Suzy is a pain in the behind," though Craig didn't sound very put out by it. He held out a hand for the wrench he'd asked Tad to hold. He was up on a ladder with his head inside the engine cowling of their HH-65 Dolphin rescue helo checking that all of the fittings were tight.

Tad ignored the waving hand and practiced twirling the wrench back and forth through his fingers. It was a move he could do in his sleep.

Craig extracted himself enough from the open cowling to look down at Tad from the top of the step ladder. "Uh-oh! I know that look."

"What look?"

"The one while you're thinking. You're a swimmer, Tad, just give it up and accept that your brain isn't your best asset."

Tad twirled the wrench a few more times just out of Craig's reach to prove that he had skills. He mis-timed Craig's reach and accidentally smacked his knuckles rather than slapping it into his crew chief's palm.

"Ow! Crap! Well, at least that proves my point."

"What point?" A voice asked from behind him.

Tad swung around to stare at Tabby standing right in his six. And he hadn't even felt her there. She was absolutely screwing with his situational awareness. Her golden hair was all stirred up. He could hear the wind that had done it, slamming against the hangar, and told himself *not* to reach out to smooth it back into place though his fingers ached to do so.

"Helo engine? Cool!" And Suzy scrambled up the back side of Craig's ladder until she was standing chest to chest with him, but all of her attention was on the engine. Or at least she was making Craig think so.

True to form, Craig fell for it and didn't notice the lush female practically pressed against him. Instead, he began walking her through the engine.

Tad wasn't quite so dense, and turned back to Tabby. "Where've you been hiding?" Still had apparently left all his smooth back in Iowa.

"I've been wondering something. How does a US Coast Guard swimmer end up coming from Iowa?" Tabby answered his question with a question.

"Lifeguard at the beach some."

"They have beaches in Iowa?"

"Aw, sure. Mine musta been most of a hundred feet long. Swimming hole dug out of the field by Old Man Jasper just off 1st Street."

"So, major surf wasn't a big deal." Damn but the woman had a great smile, slow and trending just a little sideways. Craig and Suzy had sealed up the engine cowling and were now inside the helo going over who cared about what.

"If you don't count when Fat Steve did cannonballs off the diving board, not so much. But I mighta also spent some summers with my uncle, a Coronado Beach SEAL. He had this thing about swimming skills." He was the one who'd taught Tad how to dream bigger than a haystack or a wheat field. It had set his future path forever apart from his Adair classmates and Tad blessed him every day for that.

That pulled out Tabby's rare laugh. Suzy was always on the edge of one, bursting forth at the least provocation —even now sounding from behind him. Tabby's was shy as a newborn barn cat, always lurking half out of sight.

"Where did you get *your* taste for water?"

"Local, remember?"

He smacked his forehead. Born and raised along the Columbia, looking out at some of the most beautiful and absolutely the most dangerous water in the world.

"Okay, local. So, where you been, local lady? Checking out old high school boyfriends?" *Please say no.* She was here at the airport, wasn't she?

"Oh sure. All of the most eligible guys in the world were born and raised right here in Astoria. You know all the ones who don't work the boats work the fryer at

McDonald's, right? So we've been hanging at McD's big time. Nothing else to do in this town." Her final grimace spoke volumes. He'd bet that she and Suzy had spent many high school afternoons doing just that.

"Wouldn't know about that. Adair was too small for a Macs. We've got Zipp's Pizza and the Chuckwagon. Oh, I think they've got a Subway now. *All* the hot babes in Iowa work at Subway, you know."

"Maybe we should introduce them. All your farmer girls and all our lame-o non-fisher boys."

"Deal," he reached out and she shook on it. Despite sitting knee-to-knee several times at Workers, it was the first time they'd actually touched. Her hand felt small and feminine in his, despite its strength. Rather than letting go, he turned it and looked down. "Someone's been fighting the grime." Embedded dark around the joints, and under chipped nails; good calluses, too. About the nicest hands he'd ever met.

"You've never seen six motor lifeboats as clean and shiny as the six at Cape D."

"They working you too hard?" He teased her a bit.

"Got this Boatswain's Mate thinks I should know every bolt of the boat and is shocked that I don't."

"Right, 'cause you've been here like seven whole days. He sounds like a hard ass."

"She, and you have no idea. I want to be just like her when I grow up."

No question who she was talking about. Sarah Goodwin's reputation was totally solid. "Not gonna find a better instructor than Sarah anywhere in the Coast Guard."

"If I survive it." But Tabby's smile as she recovered her hand said she was totally down with the challenge.

He'd never been much of hand holder, but he could feel the memory of her fingers curled up in his palm like a fresh-hatched chick.

TABBY'S PHONE RANG LOUD; MADE HER JUMP. SHE DIDN'T like letting anything show when she was surprised, but her mind had drifted as Tad held her hand. The raw power of the man was amazing. She could feel every bit of his immense strength—yet his control as well. He'd held her hand like he'd never let go, but not with some overtight grip.

"Hi. This is Tabby."

There was a brief pause. "This live Tabby, or recording Tabby?" BM1 Sarah Goodwin asked sharply.

"Live version." She really had to change how she answered the phone. She got that question all the time.

"Good. Where are you two?"

"Coast Guard helo hangar in Astoria."

"God damn it all to hell!" The vitriol was lethal.

"We were cleared off base, Bosun." Tabby replied carefully, hopefully a fair defense.

"I'm down a crew member and we've got an imminent rescue. Figured between you two that you could cover for him. How fast can you get here? Shit. Never mind. Forty minutes. I'm screwed and stuck at the dock."

Ten miles line-of-sight was a slow twenty-mile drive through town and then over the tall Astoria-Megler Bridge.

Even as Sarah fumed, the two pilots came rushing in. Maybe they'd gotten the rescue call as well.

Tabby had an idea. Just maybe... "Hold on, Sarah."

"For what?"

Tabby didn't answer, instead she listened.

"How fast can we get aloft?" Sly called out.

She liked that Tad and Craig barely had to exchange a glance before they answered in unison, "Three minutes."

"Do it! Your bird, Ham, get us spinning."

Tad had already stripped off his shirt as he headed to the equipment rack at the side of the hangar. Moments later he was down to tighty-whities. She knew that rescue swimmers were among the most fit of anyone in any service, but seeing it spelled out in rippling muscle across his back, butt, and legs was...

Her mind blanked.

"I know that look," Sly spoke up close beside her. "Hell, if I weren't straight and married, I'd be all over that." He bumped his shoulder against hers, then turned for his helo.

"Captain...Uh..." Tabby couldn't remember his last name. Suzy would know, of course, but she was busy watching Hammond doing the engine startup procedure.

"Captain Uh, that's me." Sly stopped and smiled at her.

"Sorry about that, sir. This is a bit presumptuous."

"Better ask quick, we're on the bounce." But he wasn't brushing her off.

"Our Bosun, Petty Officer Goodwin, is down a crew member. I'm guessing she got the same call you did. She's asked how fast we could get there."

"That her?" Sly pointed toward the phone that Tabby had completely forgotten she was holding.

Sly slipped it out of her fingers. "Sarah? Sly here. We're aloft in two; you'll have your crew in five. You owe me." He handed back the phone without waiting for an answer and waved her toward the helo's cargo bay with a grin.

"We're on our way, Sarah," she said into the phone even as she waved Suzy aboard.

"So I heard. Done good. Keep surprising me, *Seaman.*" She hit the last word hard to remind Tabby not to be too uppity in using her given name, then PO Goodwin was gone.

Tabby climbed aboard mere seconds ahead of Tad in full swimmer's gear. He now wore form-hugging International Orange neoprene, with an inflatable life vest and a small utility belt. Fins and a snorkel stuck out of a gear bag as he tugged on his helmet.

The transformation was magical. In such simple gear, he was now headed out to jump into the rough waters of the Pacific Ocean to save other people's lives. He looked...amazing!

"How far you going with us, Tabby?" He asked happily as he settled in his seat against the rear bulkhead.

"Just as far as Cape D."

Suzy grinned and rolled her eyes at her.

"Oh." Somewhere along the way she'd become the perfect fall girl for a straight line. But she hadn't been best friends with Suzy for over eighteen years and learned nothing. "Depends on how far *you* want to go, Swimmer." It wasn't the smoothest recovery, but it worked. Also, once she said it, it felt surprisingly true.

He burst out laughing as the helo lifted and Craig slammed the side doors shut. "Stick with the straight lines, pretty lady. They fit you way better."

Okay, hopefully her crew skills would be better than her so-not-Suzy flirt skills.

7

Tad saw the change come over her. Something shifted after he hit her with that off-hand tease.

She sat straighter. Gave a half nod to herself as she tugged her t-shirt smooth. She'd tried to flirt a little, and it hadn't fit her at all. Just not the person she was. Not that she was bad at it; she'd delivered the line perfectly and definitely sent his imagination to some very nice places.

But it didn't fit his *image* of her.

And if he was reading her face right—he'd become a good judge of expressions in all of his rescues—it abruptly didn't fit her own image of herself either. Not even a little.

He glanced at Suzy. She was looking at Tabby, they were sitting almost knee-to-knee on the cargo bay deck, but she wasn't seeing it. Suzy should be the one he was attracted to. Flirty and funny. Smart, but not real interested in deeper thought.

No question but Tabby was a deep thinker. And it

looked as if she just pulled it on like a skin tighter than his wetsuit.

Ham barely hesitated as the girls dumped out at Cape D. Back in the air, Tad watched them sprinting down the dock toward one of the boats.

He also noticed that Craig had slid his own seat, mounted on a side-to-side rail at the front of the cabin, so that he too could watch them run.

"What do ya think, buddy boy?"

Craig shook his head bemused. "Swears she never looked at a turboshaft engine before, but she just...got it. Somewhere inside that lovely woman is a very sharp mechanic."

Tad snorted. "That's you all over. A crew chief first and a man ninety-third. Bet you didn't even notice her pressing her chest against you up on that ladder."

Craig grinned at him. "I noticed plenty. A ladder is just a little precarious for what ideas she brought to mind. Noticed you were actually holding Tabby's hand without dragging her off to the nearest closet."

"Maybe," he shrugged. It didn't sound like him.

Then Sly came on the intercom. "If you two love birds can get some focus, we have a ship collision about ten miles northwest."

They spent the next couple minutes, as the helo raced out to sea, going over what little information was available. A fishing trawler and a coastal container ship had rammed one another in the wide-open ocean.

Neither was expected to stay afloat long.

The thick fog that always lay offshore had enveloped the wreck. It delayed them finding it for five painfully long minutes before they arrived above the tangled mess.

Tad had jumped crabbing boats of Alaska and sailboats caught in a nor'easter, but never in such weird weather. Clear blue skies above and out to the horizon. The tall Cascade Range stood out sharply against the summer sky. Below? Blowing thirty knots in a dense fog layer lumping over twenty-foot swells. Looking off to either side, the sea was invisible.

Straight down, it was a disaster.

A typical fishing trawler might have merely damaged the container ship as it was sliced in two. No such luck, the ship had rammed a fifty-meter stern trawler right up the kazoo. Rather than the bow just cutting the trawler in two, the trawler had been stout enough to sheer much of the bow off the container ship before it succumbed. The trawler was in two halves, with one of the halves already missing, probably at the bottom of the sea. And the container ship was nose-down with the foredeck awash.

Dozens of forty-foot steel shipping containers— maybe hundreds hiding within the fog—were floating about the two wrecked ships. The swells banged them together creating a floating hazard like none he'd ever seen.

"Where the hell do we begin?" Ham called over the radio.

Tad studied it for longer than his usual ten or so seconds. Long enough for Craig to make a worried sound.

The plan of attack was up to the rescue swimmer.

"How long to the next helo arriving?"

"Fifteen minutes," Sly reported. "About the same as the first MLBs."

There were rafts floating among the containers, bright orange dots. Here and there were tiny specks of crewmen in the water. They all were at risk from the debris.

Even as he watched, a pair of containers were thrown together so hard that he could hear the metal bang and crumple right over the sound of the Dolphin's twin turboshaft engines and pounding rotor.

And there were personnel still aboard both ships waving at his bird.

The Dolphin could pick up seven.

There were over thirty.

"The trawler hull is heading down first. Let's start there."

He could feel the desperation of the other seamen as the helo shifted toward the remaining half of the fishing trawler. Not everyone was coming home from this one.

Senior Chief Vernon had been clear on that. *Don't think. Act! You save every single one you can. Each one you save is one less for the sea.*

The lashing wires and tangled nets of the trawler meant they couldn't risk winching him down to the deck.

Craig called the position to Ham.

After they'd run the pre-swimmer-insertion checklist, all Tad focused on now was even-breathing and the security of his gear.

When Craig's slap landed on his shoulder, he launched feet first into the angry wreckage.

8

"Oh. My. God."

"I don't think God is helping much on this one," Sarah answered.

She and Tabby were standing side-by-side on the flying bridge of the 47-MLB. Suzy was down below checking on the engines. The boat's two rescue crew were down in the survivors' cabin—a six-seat watertight compartment directly below their feet. They were fully dressed in wetsuits and probably playing their usual gin rummy despite the rough ride.

Sarah may have been last off the line by eight minutes, but she'd sliced such a line through the surf over the Columbia River Bar that in the half an hour from Cape D, she was the lead boat.

"Wreckage at ten o'clock!" Tabby shouted and pointed off the left bow.

"Good eye," Sarah backed both engines hard. A container floated just awash, visible only as an incongruous flat spot in the wind-ripped water. "Swimmers ready?"

How was she supposed to know that?

Sarah had given them only minimal instructions as they'd raced aboard and yanked on their Mustang onsie float gear.

"Engineer got some bad fish and is blowing at both ends with food poisoning. Between you two, you're covering. Suzy, just keep my boat running. Tabby, you're my right hand. Don't even think of doing something without clearing it with me. Either of you ever unhook both of your safety lines at the same time, I'm gonna leave you behind after you're washed overboard." And that had been the end of the orientation for their first real-world rescue.

So, Tabby got ready to go find out if the swimmers were ready. They weren't rescue swimmers like Tad—technically he was an Aviation Survival Technician. The only way the MLB's swimmers were allowed off the boat was if they were tied to the MLB on a line. But they were still incredible swimmers.

She turned and would have fallen over backwards if she hadn't been harnessed into her seat—they were both standing close behind her.

"They're ready," she reported.

Sarah may have smiled; she couldn't have missed Tabby's flinch.

"Let's start with the rafts before one of them gets pancaked," Sarah shouted over the grinding scrape of a container thrown out of a wave hard enough to peel open the container they'd almost hit. It sank before she could get a look at the contents.

Tabby held her breath as a sheet of spray plowed across the bridge. Once she'd wiped her eyes, she could see two rafts. The first was closer, and the other was being batted about a floating container. She automatically pointed to the second.

"I like your instinct," Sarah shouted over the roar of the boat's engines as she fought clear of another wave. "You do remember to think safety first, right?"

"Isn't it supposed to be, 'That Others May Live'?"

"That's the swimmer's creed, not the Coast Guards'. Of course," Sarah aimed for the imperiled raft. "I've always liked that creed." Her grin was wicked as she intentionally rammed the nose of the MLB into the container, then laid in full power to shove it clear of the raft.

The boat's swimmers were back on the aft deck. She spotted them coming up on her side of the boat where the side walkway dropped within a foot of the water to aid rescues just like this.

"Swimmers on the port side," she shouted to Sarah.

"Good. Call the distances."

And she did, as they slid nearer and nearer the raft. Three faces peered out the opening in the protective canopy. Once close enough, one of the swimmers snapped a line onto the raft as the other began hauling people out of it. Two men and one woman were directed to the afterdeck. Only one man was in Mustang float gear. The woman wore standard slicks, and the last guy had little more than jeans and a jacket. He was in bad shape and had to be carried up the three steps from the rescue well.

After they double-checked the raft, the swimmers slashed its inflated sides, and released it. It sunk out of sight in moments.

"Why not recover it?" Tabby shouted as Sarah carved a hard turn for the second raft.

"You'll see."

Tabby had some theories about—

The bow of the fishing trawler shot out the front of the wave and nearly skewered them. A 47' Motor Lifeboat, not matter how tough, was no match for a hundred-and-sixty-foot section of fishing trawler.

Two helos and their swimmers were working the other side of the wreckage. Two more MLBs had arrived while they were rescuing the first raft's crew. She barely had time to hope that Tad was being safe.

They spent ten minutes dodging around, trying to reach the other raft. It was a standard eight-person octagonal with a full canopy. After each successive wave, Tabby could find no way to predict its next position.

Finally, another MLB managed to catch it.

Tabby watched as they snapped on a line, looked inside, then slashed and sank it.

"We both just spent ten minutes chasing a raft that no one had gotten into. Knew it was light by the way it skittered around, but we had to check. Could have been a kid aboard. Now we slash it so that no one else wastes any more time on it."

Tabby nodded, searched around for the next raft, and then spotted Tad.

He had emerged from the face of a wave dragging a person not twenty feet from her boat.

"Swimmer in the water!" she shouted.

Sarah slowed, backed, and lined her boat up as the wave lifted behind them.

Tabby could feel the punch through her feet as the wave picked up Tad and his rescue and slammed them into the side of the boat just below her feet.

Hopefully the loud clang was the hard slap of the wave and not Tad's head against the hull.

9

"GRAB HIM!" TAD SHOUTED WITH WHAT LITTLE AIR WAS left in his body after the hard hit.

Two hands reached down from above and grabbed the collar of the guy. Tad wasn't sure if the guy was still alive, but he'd gotten him out of the maelstrom.

His helo had been fully loaded so he'd waved them ashore. Since then he'd been swimming from body to body until he found a live one. Then he set out with everything he had left to reach the MLB he'd spotted playing a game of dodgeball with a cluster of containers.

Ten minutes of hard swimming he was nearly played out.

On the next wave, the guy he'd rescued was floated right out of his hands and up onto the flying bridge.

In moments, the guy was strapped into the spare seat behind the two pilot positions.

Then the assistant bosun looked back over the rail at him.

His ears were still ringing with his impact against the

boat. The roar of wave and engine drowned out all other sound.

But there was no mistaking the worried words forming on Tabby's lips, "You okay?"

He checked. Nothing broken despite a few spots dancing in front of his eyes.

Tad pointed two fingers to his own eyes, then at her, then out at the water. Her extra six feet of elevation would give her a better view. Cold, tired, and ringing ears weren't going to be slowing him down.

And like the warrior she was, she didn't waste a moment. Instead, she went looking. When she shot an arm out to the rear, he dove back into the water and dug hard.

For the next hour, he followed the directions of his guiding angel, seeking survivors to haul back to her boat.

10

Tabby didn't know what to say to him.

They sat at the Workers Tavern bar, just next to the four graybeards, apparently on a musical siesta as they talked about sinkings of the past—some of which must have happened before even they were born.

Twice she'd seen a survivor, but in a position so dangerous that she didn't want to point him out to Tad. But, even knowing he'd go into the nightmare and perhaps not return, she gave him the signal—and he went.

The MLB's two swimmers often jumped in and swam out to the limits of their safety lines, to save Tad having to come all the way back to the boat.

And each time, he'd look to her as he tread water for a moment, and she'd find him another target.

"Nine," he whispered softly to his beer.

"No, twenty-four. We saved twenty-four."

"Nine didn't make it."

"No," she knew where he got the line. In the movie

The Guardian, Kevin Costner played a rescue swimmer who only ever counted the lives he *hadn't* saved. It was probably the most aired movie in any Coast Guard Station.

Tad didn't look up at her.

She nudged him hard enough to make him turn to her.

"No, Tad. It doesn't work like that."

"Yeah, it does, sister."

"First, not your sister. Second, you were magnificent today. Did you save all those people because you said, 'I can't let one die.' Or did you do it because you said, 'I can save at least one more.' Go on, tell me it was the first one."

He blinked at her in surprise.

"You were..." the words caught in her throat but she didn't have any others, "...magnificent."

"I'm just a kid from Iowa."

"Who gives everything he's got to save one more person. Why are you in the Guard, Tad? I looked up your hometown. Adair is two hundred miles to the Mississippi and three hundred to Lake Michigan. How does a kid like that end up in the ocean off Astoria, Oregon?"

"How about you?" He fired it back like an accusation. "Shit! Sorry. Local girl. How many did you lose to the sea?"

"None. I've been lucky. Just turns out the sea is in my blood, even if I didn't know it."

Tad turned back to studying his half-empty beer.

Tabby didn't know how to reach him. Tad had performed magic. Of the twenty-four saves, fifteen had been Tad's, despite two other boats and another helo's rescue swimmer being on site. And all he could see was the lives he *hadn't* saved.

"Girlie," one of the graybeards whispered to her. The other three were still reliving old wrecks.

"Yeah?"

"Ask him who he lost."

She could only blink at him in surprise.

His expression was sad with knowledge.

And then she knew. She squeezed the guy's gnarled hand in thanks and turned back to Tad.

"You loved your uncle very much, didn't you?"

In answer, Tad slowly twisted his beer back and forth between those strong hands that had saved so many lives.

Tabby rested her hand on his to quiet them.

He finally nodded. "Yeah. He died on a mission, shot down in Afghanistan. A SEAL, in the middle of the fucking desert, his helo downed by an RPG. Never even had a goddamn chance to fight back. Should never have left the sea. He understood its ways like no man I've ever met. I save people because he died."

"No, Tad. You save people because of how he lived. He taught a little boy to love the sea."

Tad's hand finally went quiet under hers, as if he was frozen in place. Just as shocked as she'd been when Tad had pointed out that she wasn't some flirty chick like Suzy, who was being very cozy with Craig just now at one of the tables. No, Tabby had always survived by thinking hard and working hard—once she'd found her direction. And Tad had given that to her in the hangar just this morning.

Then he slowly returned to twirling his beer, but didn't look up at her.

She almost turned back to the graybeard to see if he had any other advice, when Tad finally spoke again.

"Craig is always saying that I'm not smart enough to be anything other than a rescue swimmer. But I'm smart enough to figure out one thing."

"What's that?"

He turned to face her and took her hand between both of his. He squeezed it tightly while he closed his eyes for a long moment. When he opened them, he looked right at her.

"What?" She could feel the pounding in her ears as her heart tried to tell her something.

"No matter what Craig says, I'm smart enough to never, ever let you out of my life, Tabby."

"But..." Tabby didn't know what to say. "We've never even kissed."

"Remember what Craig said."

She had to laugh, "Not smart enough to be anything other than the most awesome rescue swimmer ever."

"Exactly. But I'm a quick learner." And he leaned in to kiss her.

She hesitated just long enough to identify the song the graybeards started singing.

Beatle's *Yellow Submarine?*

She couldn't help giggling into Tad's kiss. No question but they were going to be stuck with *that* as their song for the rest of their lives.

LAST WORDS

I created five stories in the rich land of the US Coast Guard and feel that I explored only the tiniest edge. By the time I was done, a dozen reference books about the USCG had been added to my shelf. My computer is littered with references from the operator's manual for a 47' Motor Lifeboat, the specifications of an HH-65 Dolphin helicopter, and the official listing of every boat and aircraft in the USCG's inventory. I even took an online course about writing the USCG authentically. (Any mistakes are wholly mine.)

What did I learn from my time visiting them? The world of "The Forgotten Service" as the Coast Guard is sometimes called, embraces a level of complexity that I actually don't see in the other forces. Yes, the bigger services may have many more actual pieces moving around because of their sheer scale.

But when a Navy ship is going down, it's the Coast Guard who responds. When an Air Force or US Marine aircraft is lost at sea, the Coast Guard is often the first and last on the scene. They inspect shipping vessels for safety, and capture narco-submarines plying the open seas. They fix buoys and channel markers, break ice on the Great Lakes and in the polar oceans, and make sure everyone is at a safe distance from the floating barges bearing July 4th fireworks shows.

With less than sixty thousand men and women, they seem to be everywhere I look. They pop up in the unlikeliest of places, just going about their varied jobs. (For comparison, here are a few other active-duty numbers: Army – 471,000, Navy and Air Force – 325,000 each, Marine Corps – 180,000. In fact, the entire US Coast Guard is also small than: either the Army or Air National Guards, and even the Reserve units of every other branch of the military.)

One of the reasons I write is to learn. I love to discover how different characters will react and interact based on who they are. I also love learning about their jobs and their tools.

I feel that, in a funny way, I discovered far more about this incredible service in these five stories than I did in some services I've written multiple novels about.

I can tell you one thing for sure; you'll *always* see me waving at that orange-and-white helicopter as it flashes by overhead.

Thank you for joining me.

(And nope, I still don't know where the graybeard chorus came from, but I love them!)

Aim high!
M. L. Buchman
North Shore, MA 2020

IF YOU ENJOYED THAT,

BE SURE YOU DON'T MISS THE MIRANDA
CHASE SERIES!

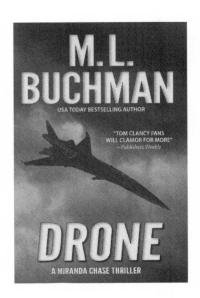

DRONE (EXCERPT)

Flight 630 at 37,000 feet
12 nautical miles north of
Santa Fe, New Mexico, USA

THE FLIGHT ATTENDANT STEPPED UP TO HER SEAT—4E—
which had never been her favorite on a 767-300. At least
the cabin setup was in the familiar 261-seat, 2-class
configuration, currently running at a seventy-three
percent load capacity with a standard crew of ten and one
ride-along FAA inspector in the cockpit jump seat.

"Excuse me, are you Miranda Chase?"

She nodded.

The attendant made a face that she couldn't interpret.

A frown? Did that indicate anger?

He turned away before she could consider the
possibilities and, without another word, returned to his
station at the front of the cabin.

Miranda once again straightened the emergency exit plan that the flight's vibrations kept shifting askew in its pocket.

This flight from yesterday's meeting at LAX to today's DC lunch meeting at the National Transportation Safety Board's headquarters departed so early that she'd decided to spend the night in the airline's executive lounge working on various aviation accident reports. She never slept on a flight and would have to catch up on her sleep tonight.

Miranda felt the shift as the plane turned into a modest five-degree bank to the left. The bright rays of dawn over the New Mexico desert shifted from the left-hand windows to the right side.

At due north, she heard the Rolls-Royce RB211 engines (quite a pleasant high tone compared to the Pratt & Whitney PW4000 that she always found unnerving) ease off ever so slightly, signaling a slow descent. The pilot was transitioning from an eastbound course that would be flown at an odd number of thousands of feet to a westbound one that must be flown at an even number.

The flight attendant then picked up the intercom phone and a loud squawk sounded through the cabin. Most people would be asleep and there were soft complaints and rustling down the length of the aircraft.

"We regret to inform you that there is an emergency on the ground. I repeat, there is nothing wrong with the plane. We are being routed back to Las Vegas, where we will disembark one passenger, refuel, and then continue our flight to DC. Our apologies for the inconvenience."

There were now shouts of complaint all up and down the aisle.

The flight attendant was staring straight at her as he slammed the intercom back into its cradle with significantly greater force than was required to seat it properly.

Oh. It was her they would be disembarking. That meant there was a crash in need of an NTSB investigator —a major one if they were flying back an hour in the wrong direction.

Thankfully, she always had her site kit with her.

For some reason, her seatmate was muttering something foul. Miranda ignored it and began to prepare herself.

Only the crash mattered.

She straightened the exit plan once more. It had shifted the other way with the changing harmonic from the RB211 engines.

———

Chengdu, Central China

AIR FORCE MAJOR WANG FAN EASED BACK ON THE joystick of the final prototype Shenyang J-31 jet— designed exclusively for the People's Liberation Army Air Force. In response, China's newest fighter jet leapt upward like a catapult's missile from the PLAAF base in the flatlands surrounding the towering city of Chengdu.

It felt as he'd just been grasped by Chen Mei-Li. Never had a woman made him feel so much like a man.

———

Keep reading at fine retailers everywhere:
Drone

ABOUT THE AUTHOR

USA Today and Amazon #1 Bestseller M. L. "Matt" Buchman started writing on a flight south from Japan to ride his bicycle across the Australian Outback. Just part of a solo around-the-world trip that ultimately launched his writing career.

From the very beginning, his powerful female heroines insisted on putting character first, *then* a great adventure. He's since written over 60 action-adventure thrillers and military romantic suspense novels. And just for the fun of it: 100 short stories, and a fast-growing pile of read-by-author audiobooks.

Booklist says: "3X Top 10 of the Year." PW says: "Tom Clancy fans open to a strong female lead will clamor for more." His fans say: "I want more now...of everything." That his characters are even more insistent than his fans is a hoot.

As a 30-year project manager with a geophysics degree who has designed and built houses, flown and jumped out of planes, and solo-sailed a 50' ketch, he is awed by what is possible. More at: www.mlbuchman.com.

Other works by M. L. Buchman: *(* - also in audio)*

Other works by M. L. Buchman:

Contemporary Romance (cont)

Where Dreams
Where Dreams are Born
Where Dreams Reside
Where Dreams Are of Christmas
Where Dreams Unfold
Where Dreams Are Written

Science Fiction / Fantasy

Deities Anonymous
Cookbook from Hell: Reheated
Saviors 101

Single Titles
The Nara Reaction
Monk's Maze
the Me and Elsie Chronicles

Non-Fiction

Strategies for Success
Managing Your Inner Artist/Writer
Estate Planning for Authors
Character Voice

Short Story Series by M. L. Buchman:

Romantic Suspense

Delta Force
Delta Force

Firehawks
The Firehawks Lookouts
The Firehawks Hotshots
The Firebirds

The Night Stalkers
The Night Stalkers
The Night Stalkers 5E
The Night Stalkers CSAR
The Night Stalkers Wedding Stories

US Coast Guard
US Coast Guard

White House Protection Force
White House Protection Force

Contemporary Romance

Eagle Cove
Eagle Cove

Henderson's Ranch
Henderson's Ranch

Where Dreams
Where Dreams

Thrillers

Dead Chef
Dead Chef

Science Fiction / Fantasy

Deities Anonymous
Deities Anonymous

Other
The Future Night Stalkers
Single Titles

SIGN UP FOR M. L. BUCHMAN'S NEWSLETTER TODAY

and receive:
Release News
Free Short Stories
a Free Book

Get your free book today. Do it now.
free-book.mlbuchman.com